THE OC
THE MISFIT

THE OC

THE MISFIT

SCHOLASTIC INC.
New York   Toronto   London   Auckland   Sydney
Mexico City   New Delhi   Hong Kong   Buenos Aires

No part of this work may be reproduced in whole or in part, or stored in a retrieval system, or transmitted in any form or by any means, electronic, mechanical, photocopying, recording, or otherwise, without written permission of the publisher. For more information regarding permission, write to Scholastic Inc., Attention: Permissions Department, 557 Broadway, New York, NY 10012.

ISBN 0-439-67700-9

12 11 10 9 8 7 6 5 4 3 2 1   4 5 6 7 8 9/0

Cover and interior designed by Louise Bova
Printed in the U.S.A.
First printing, October 2004

THE MISFIT

Adapted by Aury Wallington
Based on the television series created by Josh Schwartz
including the episode "The Rescue" story by Allan Heinberg,
teleplay by Melissa Rosenberg; the episode "The Heights"
written by Debra J. Fisher & Erica Messer; the episode "The
Perfect Couple" written by Allan Heinberg; the episode "The
Homecoming" written by Josh Schwartz and Bryan Oh; the
episode "The Secret" written by Allan Heinberg and Josh
Schwartz; the episode "The Best Chrismukkah Ever" written
by Stephanie Savage; the episode "The Countdown," written by Josh Schwartz; the episode "The Third Wheel" written by Melissa Rosenberg; the episode "The Links" written
by Debra J. Fisher & Erica Messer; the episode "The Rivals"
written by Josh Schwartz; the episode "The Truth" written
by Allan Heinberg; the episode "The Heartbreak" written by

Josh Schwartz; the episode "The Telenovela," written by Stephanie Savage; the episode "The Goodbye Girl" written by Josh Schwartz; the episode "The L.A." written by Josh Schwartz; the episode "The Nana" written by Allan Heinberg; the episode "The Proposal" written by Liz Friedman and Josh Schwartz; the episode "The Shower" written by J.J. Philbin; the episode "The Strip" written by Allan Heinberg; and the episode "The Ties That Bind" written by Josh Schwartz.

THE MISFIT

1

"You are not putting me in an insane asylum," Marissa shouted. She pulled the thin yellow hospital blanket up under her chin, shielding herself as much as possible from her mother's stare.

"It's not an *insane asylum*, it's a recovery center. For young women who are . . . troubled," Julie Cooper answered patiently, struggling to keep a smile plastered across her face. "I think, and Dr. Burke agrees, that it would be a good idea for you to have a break."

Marissa looked at her mother in horror. This was a nightmare. Pretty much her entire life had been a nightmare, ever since her father told her that her parents were separating. Getting drunk in Tijuana, taking too many prescription painkillers — as if there were a pill that existed that could end the pain she was feeling at her father's news — overdosing and nearly dying in Mexico . . . Marissa didn't know how things had gotten so out of control. How *she* had gotten so out of control.

Marissa never would have tried to commit suicide — at least not intentionally. She was just . . . sad. And drinking made the sad feelings all fuzzy and abstract, as if she were watching a movie of herself, the sort of soggy tearjerker that you use a whole box of Kleenex crying over, but can still turn off when it's done. Alcohol let her turn off her life for a little while. But she didn't want to turn it off permanently. What happened in Mexico was an accident, but no one seemed to believe her. No one, that is, except for Ryan.

He'd arrived at the hospital earlier that afternoon, clutching a ridiculous yellow sunflower that had been the only thing left at the gift shop. He'd grinned as he presented it to her, the smile on his face not quite managing to conceal the fact that he was fighting back tears.

Marissa was devastated that she'd made him cry — he'd been through so much with his own family that the last thing he needed was her causing him more problems.

"I'm sorry," she said, twirling the sunflower under her nose. The flower cast a bright, cheerful reflection on her face, making her look like she should be doing something healthy and outdoorsy, like surfing or playing volleyball on the beach, rather than sitting in a locked psych ward. "I'm sorry," she repeated, "I was so dumb. What I did —"

"Hey, come on," Ryan said. He lightly brushed his fingers across her cheek, relieved and gratified to find it warm and vibrant, and nothing like the icy pallor she'd had when he'd found her in that alley. He let his hand linger, stroking her cheek, trying to figure out a way to tell her what he was thinking.

"I didn't want to kill myself," Marissa said in a small voice. "I didn't. I just wanted to . . . escape."

"I know," Ryan said. "I get it."

Marissa gave him a tentative smile, taking his hand in hers and visibly relaxing for the first time since she'd woken up to find herself hospitalized that morning. "My mom's treating me like I'm Sylvia Plath. It's so annoying. I just want to get out of here, so everything can go back to being normal."

"Normal would be good," Ryan said, cracking a smile at the thought. Nothing had been normal for him since he'd come to the O.C. three months ago. His life was better, sure, but "normal"? Not a chance. He raised his eyebrows at Marissa, copying the expression Seth always wore whenever he found something ironic, and Marissa burst out laughing.

"Normal would be very good," she agreed, still giggling, but before Ryan could answer, they heard a voice coming from the hall. Julie's voice.

"Nurse, when you get a chance, my daughter is ready for her lunch."

"Oh my god," Ryan said, looking wildly around the room for an escape hatch. The last thing in the world that he needed was for Julie Cooper to catch him in here.

"The closet!" Marissa hissed. "Quick!"

Ryan tumbled around the bed and ducked into the closet, barely pulling the door shut behind him in time, as Julie strode into the room to tell her daughter that she was shipping her down to San Diego to stay in a mental institute.

"If you want to get rid of me that bad," Marissa shouted at her mother, "why don't you just let me stay at Dad's?"

"He's one of the things I think you need a break from," Julie said.

"*One* of the things?" Marissa asked, scowling. "Admit it, Mother. This is about Ryan."

"Fine," Julie answered, matching her daughter's scowl with one of her own. "Ever since you met that boy, you've changed."

"I haven't —" Marissa started, but Julie raised her voice, talking right over her daughter's protests.

"You tried to kill yourself!"

"That wasn't his fault," Marissa said, anxious to make her mother understand that Ryan was basically the only thing that had *stopped* her from killing herself. She glanced at the closet door, unable to bear the thought of Ryan overhearing the things Julie was saying.

"Sweetie, you keep saying that," Julie said, her voice softening. She put a hand on Marissa's arm. "But before he got here? You were happy."

Inside the closet, Ryan felt Julie's words as sharply as if she'd slapped him. He'd spent his whole life trying to make people happy. Everyone from his mother to his brother to Marissa even. Why did it always seem to go wrong in the end? Ryan couldn't understand what he'd done. What specific things he'd done that made Julie Cooper think he was ruining her daughter's life. And yet, according to her, he was, which would make him really . . . awful.

Only? The thing was, somehow, Ryan didn't really believe it. If he was that much of an asshole, how come Sandy liked him? And Kirsten? They didn't seem worried that he would ruin their lives. They didn't even blame him that much for burning down Kirsten's model home. Although he'd only been living with the Cohens for a few short months, he already was beginning to feel . . . worthwhile. Like he mattered. Like maybe, just maybe, he'd actually found his home.

Then again, if Julie Cooper had anything to say about it, maybe not.

Ryan wasn't sure what he'd done to incur her wrath, but he was willing to face it, if it meant he could be with Marissa. No matter how much she hated him, she couldn't drive him away. He only hoped Marissa agreed.

"Look," Julie said, carefully arranging her lips back into the smile that she found so hard to maintain around her daughter lately, "Dr. Burke will be here after lunch. Please just talk to her, honey. Let her help you. Okay?"

Marissa nodded, blinking her eyes a few times and stretching sleepily, willing to try anything to get her mom out of the room. She snuggled down under the blanket, gazing drowsily at Julie. "I'm going to nap for a while," she murmured.

Julie leaned close to Marissa, kissing the air over her daughter's forehead. "You get your rest, sweetie. I'll be back to check on you later."

The second Julie was gone, Marissa scrambled out of bed and opened the closet door, already apologizing. "I'm so sorry about that. Her."

"It's okay," Ryan said, staring down at the floor. "I should go, anyway."

"Ryan." Marissa put her hand on his arm and moved closer to him, so close that she could feel the heat radiating off him, sending little prickles of electricity between their bodies. She was suddenly, hugely conscious of the fact that she was wearing only a thin cotton hospital gown and nothing else, but she didn't let go of his arm, shifting even closer to him, as close as she could possibly get without actually touching.

Ryan let his eyes meet hers for a long moment and then dropped them, deliberately taking in her half-clothed body. "Nice outfit," he said, with a joking leer.

Marissa laughed again, playfully shoving him away. "Ryan! Get out of here."

"Okay, but I'll be back. As soon as I can."

"I don't know," Marissa said, turning serious again. "My mom —"

"I'm not afraid of your mom," Ryan said.

"Well, I am," she answered. She meant it as a joke, but it was the least funny thing she'd ever said.

2

Ryan was late to meet Sandy and Kirsten at the Harbor School for his appointment with the principal. By the time he'd skirted Julie Cooper and biked over to the campus, he was out of breath and his sweat-soaked shirt was sticking to his back.

"Sorry," he mumbled, sliding onto the bench where the Cohens sat, impeccably groomed and looking completely at ease.

"How is Marissa?" Kirsten asked, unable to stop herself from reaching over and smoothing down Ryan's hair.

Ryan shrugged, squirming away from her touch. "She's okay, I guess. She's awake and talking."

"And how are you doing, kiddo?" Sandy asked.

Ryan grunted noncommittally, staring at the floor.

Sandy looked at him. "Good to hear!" he said, affectionately rumpling the hair that his wife had just tamed.

God, Ryan liked the Cohens. He'd never known before he met them that adults could be so relaxed

7

and smart and funny, while still staying totally in control. He felt safe around Kirsten and Sandy, in a way he could hardly ever remember feeling before. It was like when he was little, before his brother started getting into trouble and his mom escaped into a bottle every night. Every once in a while, his mom would come into his room at bedtime, but instead of turning out the lights after she tucked him in, she'd give him a flashlight, and whatever library book he was currently devouring, and a stack of Oreos, and Ryan would stay up reading as late as he wanted, all night sometimes. That's how living at the Cohens' house made him feel all the time. Trusted, and secure, and all tucked in.

He smiled at the Cohens now, again silently cursing whatever social disability he had that kept him from telling people he liked how much he appreciated them. Maybe he could send them an e-mail. Or stick a Post-it on the refrigerator. But before they could smile back or say anything, he turned his attention away, to the principal's closed office door.

Kirsten followed his gaze. "Everything's going to be fine," she told him.

Ryan shifted nervously in his seat. "It's just . . . at Chino Hills, you just kind of showed up. No interviews. No essays. Just make it through the metal detector and you were in."

"Ryan," Kirsten said, giving him an encouraging pat on his leg, "the Harbor School is one of the best private schools in the country. If you graduate from here, you can get into any college in the state."

"I have to get in here first," Ryan said, looking around for a water fountain. There wasn't one. He slumped back in his seat, wondering why he was finding it so hard to swallow.

"You'll get in," Sandy boomed. "Once Dr. Kim talks to you, she'll realize what a bright kid you are."

"Oh god," Ryan groaned, then seemed surprised that he'd said that out loud.

"What?" Sandy asked.

"Dr. Kim? Seth says she's a little . . ."

"What?" Sandy repeated.

Ryan made his hands into claws and hissed like a tiger at Sandy and Kirsten. The adults laughed.

"That's about right," Sandy said, nodding.

"Shhh . . ." Kirsten whispered, but before they could get themselves together, the door opened and Dr. Kim herself appeared.

"Please come in," she said in a dignified voice, gesturing for them to follow her into the office.

They did, Sandy making one last tiger-swipe at Ryan. The boy grinned, and Sandy put a warm hand on his shoulder as they went to face Dr. Kim.

"Not exactly Harbor School material," Dr. Kim said. She'd been studying Ryan's folder for the better

9

part of an hour, shaking her head and clucking over each of Ryan's former infractions, while Kirsten, Sandy, and Ryan all squirmed in front of her.

She closed the folder and slid it across the desk toward them. They looked down at it, but nobody moved to pick it up. "Perhaps a place like Redondo Central would be a better fit for a student with Ryan's background," Dr. Kim continued.

"My background?" Ryan asked incredulously.

Dr. Kim nodded once, then shifted in her chair, embarrassed.

"I can't change where I'm from. But I can change where I'm going," he told her.

"Ryan's had a lot to overcome," Sandy added, "but in the right environment, he could really excel."

"There's no doubt that Mr. Atwood has extraordinary promise," Dr. Kim agreed. "But if he fails here, he could lose a year of school. Not to mention his self-confidence."

"With all due respect," Ryan said, leaning across the table and addressing her directly, "if you think not letting me in is going to give me self-confidence . . ." He smiled, mustering all his charm. "Come on. Give me a shot." As politely as he could, he slid the folder back across to Dr. Kim's side of the table.

Dr. Kim looked from Ryan's hopeful face to Sandy's and Kirsten's pleading ones and sighed. "One shot. That's all."

"So I'm in?" Ryan asked, his grin growing wider.

"You're in," Dr. Kim said.

"We're in!" Kirsten shrieked and, throwing her arms around Ryan, gave him a smooch on the cheek. Sandy thumped him happily on the back, and for once, Ryan didn't even try to move away from their touch.

3

"Your mother tells me you struggled with anorexia in the ninth grade."

Dr. Burke, the psychiatrist who held Marissa's fate in her perfectly manicured hands, lowered her clipboard and stared at Marissa, waiting for a response.

"I was just stressed," Marissa said, trying not to sound sullen or depressed. If she could get this woman to like her, maybe she would take Marissa's side against Julie, and she wouldn't have to get shipped off to the institution. "My mother hasn't eaten a carbohydrate in five years. *I'm* not the one with the problem."

Dr. Burke stared at her for a minute, then wrote something on her clipboard. Marissa watched her, convinced she was blowing it.

"And is that when you started drinking?"

"I guess so," Marissa answered softly.

"Would you say you drink a lot?"

"Back then? No. Not at all."

"What about now?"

Marissa was silent. Whatever she said would only be used as ammunition against her. If they knew how much she'd come to rely on a couple of swigs of whatever she could steal from the liquor cabinet just to make it through the day, they'd ship her away for sure. But Marissa had a funny feeling that Dr. Burke would be able to see the truth even if she lied.

After a minute, Dr. Burke looked back down at her clipboard and moved on to the next question on the list.

"Let's talk about your home life. A lot of things going on right now."

Marissa shrugged.

"Your father being indicted. Bankruptcy. Your parents separating. That's a lot to handle, am I right?"

Marissa nodded, still afraid to meet the psychiatrist's eyes.

"I bet home is probably the last place you want to be right now," Dr. Burke said in a casual voice.

Marissa could feel the tears filling her eyes, threatening to overflow at any second. And she had a terrible feeling that once she started crying, she wouldn't ever be able to stop. But something had to give — if she held it all in one second longer, she would explode into a million pieces, so she opened her mouth and said, "Yes."

"Yes?" Dr. Burke repeated, still in that super-casual voice.

"Home is the last place I want to be."

* * *

13

"All right, buddy, you and me," Seth said, grinning at Ryan. "Look out, Harbor School. It's the two *compañeros*. Butch and Sundance. Batman and Robin . . ."

"Mary-Kate and Ashley," Summer said, joining the boys on their bench outside the Harbor bookstore. She picked up Seth's stack of textbooks and dumped them unceremoniously in his lap, then slumped down next to him with a heavy sigh.

"Thank you," Seth said, wincing. "Sharp corners, you know, are not good. . . ."

"What's going on?" Ryan interrupted.

Summer turned to face him, her eyes wide. "I need your help."

"Absolutely," Seth said, nodding a whole bunch of times. "What do you need? I'll do it."

Summer glanced at him, then angled her body away from him, addressing herself solely to Ryan.

"Coop just called. She's freaking. Her mom's threatening to send her off to an insane asylum."

"Yeah, I heard," Ryan said, his face grim.

"No way," Seth breathed. "That's crazy. I mean, she can't do that."

"Well, she's going to. She's signing the papers at five o'clock."

"Not if I have anything to say about it," Ryan said. He leaped to his feet and, slinging his books into his backpack, got onto his bike. "Let's go!"

Seth and Summer gave each other a look as Ryan started to pedal away.

"I have a car," Summer called after him, working hard to keep the mockery out of her voice.

Without missing a beat, Ryan hopped off his bike and started moving toward Summer's car. "Let's go!" he barked at the others.

Seth and Summer shared another glance. "I guess we're going," Summer said.

"What are you wearing?" Seth asked Summer. The pink-and-white candy striper's outfit that on other girls looked so sweetly adorable gave Summer a distinct resemblance to a Naughty Nurse, like the ones featured in Seth's sole piece of porn, a tattered *Hustler* from 1986.

Unable to think about that, Seth grabbed a book off the cart and began flipping through it.

"Shut up, Cohen," Summer said. "My candy striper outfit is what got us in here in the first place." She glanced down at the book he was holding. "And don't be gross with Madame Bovary. Or *you'll* be the one eating arsenic."

"You've read Flaubert?"

"Five times," Summer answered.

"You're a strange and mysterious girl, Summer," Seth told her.

But before Summer could answer, they spotted Julie Cooper breezing down the hall, Dr. Burke in tow.

"Go get Ryan," Summer whispered to Seth. "I'll run interference."

As Seth sped down the hall toward Marissa's room, Summer wheeled her book cart up to Julie.

"Hi, Mrs. Cooper. How's Marissa?"

"She'll be fine," Julie answered. "Eventually."

Summer looked anxiously from Julie's face to Dr. Burke's. "Are you her doctor?"

"I'm her therapist," Dr. Burke said.

"Oh, thank god. You have to help me!" Summer grabbed Dr. Burke's arm to stop her from walking away. Julie stopped, too, unwilling to alienate another one of Marissa's friends.

"What's wrong?" Dr. Burke asked in a kind voice.

"Uh, I keep having this dream. About snakes! And, um . . . tunnels!" Summer looked back and forth at the two women, her expression innocent. "What could it possibly mean?"

"Maybe you should make an appointment and find out," Julie told her. "But now we need to get going. It was nice of you to come visit Marissa."

"But wait! You can't go!" Summer shouted. She gave the book cart a push so it rolled in Julie's path, blocking her from the hallway to Marissa's room.

"Why not?" Julie asked, her eyes narrowing. "Summer, what is going on?"

Summer stammered, looking around wildly for anything to rescue her from having to answer, and found her salvation in . . . Seth, who was walking down the hall, smiling at her.

"Come on, Summer, these books won't deliver themselves," he said, grabbing her arm and steering her down the hall in the opposite direction from which he'd come. "Nice to see you again, Mrs. Cooper," he called over his shoulder as he and Summer rounded the corner and disappeared from sight.

Julie watched them go, then turned on her heel and strode down the hall, to Marissa's empty room.

In the stairwell leading down to the ground floor of the hospital, Ryan turned his back to give Marissa privacy while she slipped out of her nightgown and into Summer's spare candy striper outfit.

"We've made it this far, we could just keep going," Ryan said, only half joking. "I have friends in Chino. We could stay with them. . . ."

"My mom would have you arrested for kidnapping and have me committed for good."

"Look," Ryan said, "if your mom's doing all this just to keep me away from you —" He paused, having trouble swallowing for the second time that day. "— I'll stay away."

"No," Marissa said, shaking her head. "I don't want that. So . . . what are we going to do?"

Ryan looked at her, his mind racing. "Ask for help," he finally said, and, taking Marissa's hand, led her down the stairs to freedom.

4

"What are you doing here?" Julie Cooper asked Ryan, closing the front door of her house partway, just in case he tried to get in.

"I need to talk to you," Ryan said calmly.

"Good," Julie said, "because I have something to say to you, too. Since you showed up, Marissa's been a wreck. Coming home crying. Having problems with her boyfriend. Fighting with me. And now you have another shining accomplishment to add to your list. In addition to stealing cars and burning down houses, you almost killed my daughter!"

Ryan kept his face calm, but his knuckles were white, his fingernails digging into his clenched fists, trying to keep his hands steady. He knew if he lost control in front of Julie Cooper, it would destroy any chance he had with Marissa forever. But at the same time he couldn't let Julie believe that he was at fault for what happened in Mexico.

"You can blame me all you want," he said in a careful, steady voice, "but I would never do anything to hurt Marissa."

"You're not going to get the chance," Julie said, her voice triumphant. "Because you're never going to see her again. You even try, and I'll make sure you get thrown back in juvie where you belong."

She started to close the door, but Ryan put out a hand to stop her. "That wasn't what I wanted to say."

Julie looked at him, waiting.

"Marissa is at the Cohens'. Sandy and Kirsten said to tell you. If you want to come over."

Julie pushed past Ryan, her eyes flashing. She pulled the front door shut, carefully locking it in front of him, then strode across her lawn to retrieve her daughter.

"Julie! How nice to see you," Sandy said, holding the door open and quickly stepping out of the way as Julie stormed past him into the house.

"Where is she? Where is my daughter?" Julie demanded. She shrugged off the placating hand Kirsten put on her arm and whirled to face them. "You might be in the habit of picking up strays, but Marissa has a home and she's coming back to it this minute."

"She doesn't want to go with you," Ryan said, appearing in the doorway. He and Julie locked eyes, mutual loathing apparent on their faces.

"You don't know what she wants," Julie said.

"I know better than you do."

"Ryan," Sandy said, giving him a look that

made Ryan swallow back the curses he wanted to shout at Julie. Sandy turned to Julie, speaking to her as gently as he could.

"I know you've been through a lot. Marissa gave us all a scare. But you've got to listen to what she's trying to tell you."

"And what is that, exactly?" Julie asked, skepticism heavy in her voice.

"I don't want to go home with you," Marissa said, appearing in the hallway behind Kirsten.

"Honey, you don't mean that," Julie said, holding her arms out to her daughter. But Marissa didn't move.

"Yes I do. I know you're only trying to help, but you're just making everything worse. I'm sorry about what happened, and I'll even see a therapist if you want me to, but I don't want to go to the hospital in San Diego."

"But honey, if you don't want to go home and you won't go to the hospital, where will you stay? Certainly not here," Julie said, glancing witheringly around the room. Sandy and Kirsten exchanged a look: *Thanks, Julie. Thanks a lot.*

"She'll stay with me." Jimmy Cooper appeared behind Marissa, putting an arm around her shoulders. Marissa leaned into her dad, giving her mother an imploring look.

"Please, Mom. I want to stay with Dad."

Julie looked around, from her daughter and ex-husband to the Cohens, who were studying the floor, to Ryan, who gazed right back at her. "Well, you all planned this out nicely, didn't you? You got me right where you want me."

"Julie, it isn't like that —" Kirsten started, but Julie stopped her.

"You want to stay with your father, that's fine," Julie said. "But this isn't over, Marissa. You can bet on that."

And she stalked to the door, slamming it behind her.

Ryan and Marissa looked at each other. Even though she had gotten exactly what she wanted, Marissa didn't feel like celebrating. In fact, she felt worse than ever, and didn't know why. The one thing she did know? She could really use a drink.

5

"This year is going to be different. Better," Seth said, looking over the wide green lawns of the Harbor School campus. He took a deep breath and smiled at Ryan. "It even smells different. Can you smell it?"

Ryan gave Seth a look: *Are you kidding?* Seth ignored him, happily chattering away as the two boys walked along the outdoor path.

"Every year since . . . well, *every* year, I come to school and sit alone, eat lunch alone, study alone. The only time anybody talks to me is when the water polo team pees in my shoes."

"They what?"

"It's a tradition. A very, very unpleasant tradition." Seth frowned for a second, then lit up. "But this year is going to be different, because I have you! And if anyone tried to pee in your shoes, you'd do that thing with your fists and they'd back off. So my thinking is that once people see us together, they'll realize I'm not a total loser, and we'll both be cooler by association. What do you think?"

As Seth looked to Ryan for an answer, a mammoth water polo dude who was coming up the path toward them checked Seth with his shoulder hard, sending him stumbling off the path, flailing for balance.

Seth righted himself, rubbing his shoulder and wincing, then picked up the book he'd dropped and smiled at Ryan. "See? That could have been a lot worse. It's working already."

Ryan looked at his grinning friend and rolled his eyes. "We're doomed."

"I should have stayed home," Marissa said. She waited by Summer's car as Summer touched up her lip gloss, looking around at the groups of girls sneaking glances at her and whispering. "Everyone's talking about me."

"Are you kidding? I bet no one even knows what happened."

"So they're going to make up stuff! That's even worse!"

Summer shook her head, slamming the car door closed and locking it. "Uh-uh, you want to know what's *worse*? Seth Cohen!"

Marissa looked up to see Seth coming toward them, with Ryan at his side. She smiled at Ryan, feeling better already.

"Hi, Marissa. Summer," Seth said, giving Summer his best smile.

"Cohen," Summer said, becoming superinterested in putting her car keys in her purse.

"What's your first class?" Marissa asked Ryan.

"Um, trigonometry with Mr. Corcetti," Ryan said, studying the crumpled slip of paper in his hand.

"Me, too. Come on, I'll show you where it is."

The two of them started down the walkway. Seth looked at their retreating backs, surprised.

"Hey! I'm going there, too!" he called, but before he could run after them, Summer poked his shoulder hard.

"Take a hint, Cohen. They want to be alone."

Seth grinned. "Well, I guess that leaves it to me to walk you to your class. Shall we?"

Summer sighed. "If we have to."

Farther up the path, Marissa and Ryan were walking along side by side. Ryan wanted to take her hand, but wasn't sure if she wanted him to. Just because she was broken up with Luke didn't mean for sure that she was ready to start dating him. Besides, Ryan didn't know if holding hands was even permitted at a school like this. Back in Chino, kids would practically be doing it in the halls between classes, but for all he knew, at Harbor PDA might get you thrown in detention or something. So he would have to make do with feeling her arm occasionally bumping against his, and feeling her breath on his cheek when she leaned in to talk to him. For now, that would have to be enough.

"I wish we could just skip school altogether," Marissa said. "We could get in my car and head out to the beach, get lunch on the pier, just hang out somewhere where all these people wouldn't be looking at me."

"I think they're looking at *me*," Ryan said, trying to ignore all the eyes following their progress down the path.

"You didn't try to kill yourself," Marissa said.

"Yeah, well you didn't get locked up in juvie."

"Okay, you win."

They laughed, feeling better about their mutual social leprosy, and Ryan dared to let his fingers brush Marissa's. That was almost as good as holding hands. Almost.

"So, what do you think? Should we get in your car and go?" he asked.

"I wish. But I can't afford to get in any more trouble."

"Yeah, Dr. Kim wasn't too happy about letting me in here. I better not give her any excuses to kick me out."

"We could do something tonight, though," Marissa said. "I have to pick up some clothes from my mom's house anyway. I could come by the pool house and say hi."

"Something to look forward to," Ryan said, and as they reached their classroom, he did take Marissa's hand, just for a second, just to say thanks.

Behind them, Seth and Summer were straggling toward the building. Seth had appropriated Summer's class schedule and was busy making plans.

"So I was thinking," he said, in a supercasual

voice, "since we both have AP Bio fourth period, maybe we should plan a little fifth-period study group. You know, we could sit under the trees, eat lunch together, talk about the mysteries of the human body. . . ."

"And exactly why would I do this with you?" Summer asked. Sure, Seth had really helped out with the whole Marissa thing, and he did look a tiny bit adorable in his goofy *Tron* T-shirt, but come on. She had standards to uphold.

"Hey," Seth said, hurt creeping into his voice. "I thought we turned a corner in Mexico."

"We aren't in Mexico anymore," she said.

"Well, that's just mean."

"Cohen —" Summer started, in an aggravated voice, but behind him, another voice also said "Cohen!" except this one actually sounded happy.

Seth and Summer turned around to see a cute girl with spiky blond hair walking toward them.

"Anna!" Seth exclaimed, wrapping his arms around her in a hug. "What are you doing here?"

"I transferred from Pittsburgh," she told him, grinning.

"So you're going to be going to Harbor. Pretty cool," Seth said. "Summer, you remember Anna?"

"How could I forget?" Summer said. She looked the other girl up and down, taking in her black hip-huggers, Pucci knockoff shirt, and arms full of retro bangles. There was something about this girl she instinctively didn't like. Maybe it was the fact that Seth seemed to like her so much. "We're going to be late for class," she told Seth impatiently.

"Anna, what do you have first period?"

"Trig."

"Perfect! We can all sit together." And ignoring Summer's angry look, Seth led the two girls into the building.

Dr. Kim was right, Ryan thought, surreptitiously wiping his sweating palms on his jeans. He wasn't Harbor School material, not by a long shot. He'd only been in school for five hours, and he was already so far behind the other kids he didn't think he'd ever catch up.

These weren't students, they were robots. They all seemed to know everything before the teacher had a chance to teach it. Before the teacher could even finish a question, he was surrounded by a sea of waving hands. And who ever heard of giving homework on the very first day of school? In American History, the teacher even gave them a test! A test on the first day of school! It was nuts.

Back in Chino, Ryan had found school almost too easy. If he hadn't been so bored by all the subjects, he would have easily been at the top of his class. But even though he got lousy grades, he still understood everything that was being taught. He felt like he'd learned.

But at Harbor, none of that knowledge was doing him a bit of good. Spanish class at his old school consisted of writing out the conjugations of endless strings of verbs. *Hablo, hablas, habla. Estudio, estudias, estudia.* Ryan could do that in his sleep. But in Senor Osorio's class, all they did was have conversations in Spanish, no English allowed. Ryan's conversational skills were pretty much limited to ordering burritos and singing along with "La Bamba"; he'd never made the leap from the words on the page to actually speaking the language. How was he ever going to pass this class?

But the worst was English Lit. Seth had neglected to tell Ryan that there was a summer reading list, so Ryan had about eight thousand pages of reading to do just to catch up, let alone the new books they were reading in class. And these were some pretty goddamn serious books. In tenth grade at Chino, the class had read *The Outsiders, A Separate Peace,* and a book of stories by Ray Bradbury. The reading list here had over twenty books on it, almost half of which he'd never even heard of. *The Crying of Lot 49? The Grass Is Singing? A Day in the Life of Ivan Denisovitch?* Ryan couldn't even pronounce it, let alone get it read in time for the first exam.

As the bell rang and Ryan gathered the pile of books in front of him, he realized that with all the work he had to do, he might not have time to see Marissa that night. In fact, he might not have time to do anything ever again!

* * *

In the biology lab down the hall, Seth's theory that this year would be different was proving itself to be true.

"So, Cohen, you're like, a good dissector, right?" Summer asked, dubiously eyeing the pan with the heavy dead frog pinned down on the wax inside.

"Hands of a surgeon," Seth answered, his cool tone completely belying the fact that inside he was jumping up and down with glee. This was the first time ever that Summer had spoken to him first.

"It's decided, then. You'll be my lab partner. And you'll write up all the boring lab reports, right?"

Seth couldn't think of anything he'd enjoy more. "Abso —" he started, when Anna, who was seated on his other side, watching this whole exchange with disgust, leaned across and put her hand on Seth's arm, pulling him away from Summer.

"Actually, Seth already promised himself to me," she said.

Seth looked at her, confused. He was about to protest, but Anna made her eyes very wide, trying to tell him — what? Seth glanced at Summer and got it. Summer was pouting, looking at Anna with an emotion that if Seth wasn't Seth and Anna wasn't Anna, he might actually mistake for jealousy.

"Sorry, Summer," he said, "I'm already betrothed."

"Whatev," Summer said, flouncing over to another desk and slamming her books down next to Jordan Cyphers, who was the only kid at Harbor who was possibly smarter, and less popular, than Seth himself.

Seth watched her go, then turned to Anna, delighted.

Anna shot him a wink, then held her hand out, using her best ER protocol. "Scalpel?"

Seth passed it to her, snapping on rubber gloves and inching the worm tray closer to her. "Where shall we begin?"

"The heart," Anna said, giving him a smile that said more than *let's-be-friends*.

At the table behind them, Summer watched, for the first time in her life completely disarmed.

When class ended, Seth was so wrapped up in his debate with Anna over whether or not Bright Eyes was the new Morrissey, that he walked right past Summer, who was standing by the door actually considering taking him up on his lunch-under-a-tree offer.

"Cohen!" she said, shocked that for the first time ever, Seth was paying attention to a girl other than her. But Seth didn't hear her. And as she watched him walking away from her down the hall, playfully bumping hips with Anna, Summer realized that forget Marissa — she was the one who seriously needed therapy. Jealous over Seth Cohen? Unbelievable!

Walking down the hall, Anna bumped Seth

back, fiddling with the cap of her pen so she'd have something to do with her hands.

"You know, you just totally blew off Summer."

"What?" Seth stopped in his tracks, starting to turn around, but Anna grabbed him.

"Don't you dare go back there."

"But it's *Summer*," he said. "I never blow off Summer."

"Well, that's your problem," Anna told him. "Girls don't like guys who are always there. They want a little bit of a chase. If you really want Summer" — she said this like she couldn't possibly believe it to be true — "you'll back off."

"You're a girl," Seth said, enlightenment striking.

"Thanks for noticing."

"Ha. No, seriously. You could give me advice. Train me in the ways of women."

"Help you get Summer? I don't know," Anna said.

Clueless, Seth gave her a kiss on the side of her head. "Thank you, thank you, thank you," he said. "This is going to be great!"

"It'll be something," Anna muttered, but followed him down the hall anyway, happy that, at least for the time being, she'd be the one eating lunch with him under a tree.

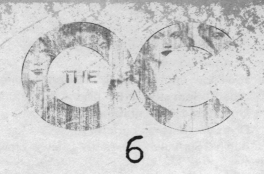

6

Ryan was up to his ears in dead Russians when the sound of the pool house door opening made him look up. Marissa, wearing a pink skirt and a pale halter top, slipped inside, her face lighting up at the sight of him.

"Hi," she said, stopping just inside the door.

"Hey," Ryan said. "Were you at your mom's?"

"Yeah, but she wasn't home, thank god. I haven't seen her since that night when we were here." She took another step, she was almost at the bed now, and looked at the book in Ryan's hand. "What are you reading?"

"Solzhenitsyn."

"Oh, I had to read that last year. It's so sad."

"What's sad is me trying to get past the first chapter," Ryan said wryly. "I can't tell any of the characters apart. And we have a test on it this Friday."

"I could help you, if you wanted," Marissa said. "Or, you know, if you needed a break . . ."

"Oh god, I would love to, but I really need to get some of this work done —" Ryan didn't want to hurt Marissa's feelings, but if he didn't get caught up, there was no way he'd make it at Harbor. "I'm so sorry, I know we had plans. . . ."

"No, that's okay," Marissa said, feeling like an idiot. She started backing toward the door, but Ryan stood up and stopped her, catching her hand.

"I really want to spend time with you. But I just —" He gestured at the stacks of work covering every surface.

"Really, it's okay. I should get home anyway, see my dad," she said vaguely.

"Maybe this weekend we could do something?" Ryan asked.

"I can't — I'm the social chair for the carnival fund-raiser — I have to be there both nights."

"I could go with you," Ryan said, and was gratified by the sudden brightness of her smile.

"Can't wait," Marissa said, opening the door. "Bye."

"See you tomorrow," Ryan said, and picked up his book again. But if concentrating had been hard before, now it was nearly impossible. Maybe he should go after Marissa, make sure she was really okay with him canceling on her. He was halfway to putting on his jacket when the pool house door opened again. He smiled, anticipating Marissa, but it was Sandy who appeared, carrying a steaming cup of coffee.

"How did it go today?" Sandy asked, setting the mug down on the bedside table.

"Not good," Ryan said, abandoning his book altogether. "I don't think it's a good idea, me in private school."

"You're one of the smartest kids they've got," Sandy said, clapping him warmly on the shoulder. "Hang in there. You'll show them all."

Ryan looked at Sandy. His whole life he had wanted to hear words like that. He had only vague memories of his father, but he'd always had the secret fantasy that his dad would have been someone like Sandy. That if he hadn't ended up in jail, he would have been supportive and kind and understanding. Probably not, though. His dad was more likely to be a bigger, older clone of Ryan's brother, Trey, well-meaning but ultimately destined for trouble. There probably wasn't a chance in hell Ryan's father was half the man that Sandy was.

Ryan looked at Sandy, who was still smiling reassuringly at him, and felt an overwhelming urge to hug him. But instead he just picked up the coffee, sipped it, and said "thanks," as if the caffeine were all he was thankful for.

When Marissa left Ryan's house, she sat in her car at the foot of her mother's driveway, trying to figure out what to do next.

Summer was busy that evening, playing hostess at a party her father was throwing for some clients, and wouldn't be able to slip away. All Marissa's other friends had been acting funny ever since Mexico — none of them had even come to visit her in the hospital! And while she knew, or at least hoped, that things would eventually get back to normal with them, she was too worn out from trying to appear happy and healthy all day to have to keep up appearances tonight. There was no way in the world she wanted to see Luke, and that, Marissa realized, was the sum total of people she knew. She guessed she would just head home. Maybe her dad would want to go see a movie or something. Marissa was definitely not the sort of person who was embarrassed to be seen out with her parents. At least with her dad, anyway.

But when she got home, instead of her father she found a twenty-dollar bill with a Post-it on it that said *For pizza. Home late. Don't wait up.*

Shit. Maybe she should follow Ryan's example and get a jump start on her schoolwork. But after she'd been staring at the first problem in her trig book for twenty minutes, she realized it was pointless to try to get any work done that night. She was too preoccupied to concentrate.

What if there really was something wrong with her? Not just about OD-ing, but in general. Shouldn't she be happy? These were her carefree teen years. So why did she feel so . . . burdened? Lots of kids had parents going through divorces. Lots of girls found out their boyfriends were cheating. The little things wrong with her didn't seem to be enough to add up to the weight of sadness she always felt.

35

As awful as it was that her mom was still going to make her see a psychiatrist, maybe it wasn't such a bad idea. A doctor would be able to tell her whether or not she was as crazy as she felt most of the time. Talking to someone whom she didn't need to impress might actually be a relief.

Marissa looked at the money her dad had left. She really should eat something. Maybe later. Instead she walked into the kitchen and opened the freezer. There were four bottles of Grey Goose vodka inside, two of which were opened. She pulled one out, got a drinking glass out of the cupboard, and poured a good three inches of liquor into it. She thought about filling the bottle the rest of the way with water so her dad wouldn't notice, but decided to risk it. Besides, she knew a kid who had replaced the missing alcohol with water so often that when he put the bottle back in his parents' freezer, the water froze solid.

Marissa looked in the fridge for something to mix it with, orange juice or some Sprite or something. What she discovered was that she and her dad really needed to go to the grocery store. Oh well. When vodka was that cold, you couldn't really taste it anyway. You sure could feel it, though. Marissa winced as the first gulp burned going down. After that it was better. By the time she finished that glass and poured herself a second, she didn't feel anything at all.

7

The next morning did not start out well for Marissa. She woke up late, not really hungover but with the sort of fuzzy depression that made her want to get back under the covers and sleep until it went away. But Jimmy had gotten up early and run out for lattes and her favorite French toast bagels, and it would have involved way too much heartbreak to explain to him exactly why she didn't think she could return to Harbor ever again.

So she pulled on her clothes and dragged herself to school. She was still fighting with the combination on her locker, long after the rest of the students had made it to their classrooms and the tardy bell rang, when who did she see coming down the hall toward her? Luke.

He stopped when he saw her, then raised a tentative hand in greeting. Already feeling the tears rising in her eyes, Marissa gave up on her locker and fled into the nearest classroom, which was thankfully deserted.

But Luke was hot on her heels.

"We need to talk, Marissa," he said, reaching for her.

Marissa yanked herself away before he could touch her. "Believe me, you do not want to hear what I have to say."

"Then will you listen to me?" he asked pleadingly.

"What, to tell me you're sorry? Forget it, Luke. You can be as sorry as you want, but I don't forgive you. I don't."

"I never meant to hurt you. I swear."

"But you did. You humiliated me, and I hate you for that, Luke, I really do."

Luke sat down heavily in a chair, his chin drooping. "Please. I just — I'm so sorry." He raised his head to look at her, and Marissa was horrified to see tears coursing down his cheeks. She had seen Ryan fighting to control his emotions and had been touched, but Luke crying? Just seemed wrong. Wrong and completely disquieting. As much as she wanted to hold her grudge, Marissa found herself willing to do almost anything to get him to stop.

"Luke, it's fine," she said uncomfortably, her finger twirling knots in her hair.

"No it's not," he said, his voice choked with sobs. "You're my best friend. You always have been. And I don't know what I'm going to do without you."

Marissa looked down at the ground, out the window, at the leftover words on the blackboard — anything to keep from having to look at his face.

Luke scooted his chair closer to her, looking for any sign that she could forgive him.

"Just because I ruined everything, it doesn't mean that I don't love you. Because I do, Marissa, I love you."

Outside the classroom, in the hallway, Ryan was walking back from the registrar's office, where he had just switched into a less-advanced Spanish class. He heard voices and peered into the classroom, just in time to hear Luke tell Marissa he loved her.

Ryan froze, his jaw working. What should he do? His gut told him to burst in there, pummel Luke until he was incoherent and bloody, kiss Marissa so long and so good that there wouldn't be any possible question in her mind who the right man for her actually was. But in his three months living in the O.C., Ryan had come to realize that every time he followed his instincts, he only made things worse. So he did the opposite of what he felt. He did nothing — just walked away, so by the time Marissa answered Luke, telling him that she no longer loved him, that it was over between them for good, Ryan was already gone.

8

The end of the school day . . . finally. Marissa stared into her locker, trying to figure out what she needed to take home. Eventually, she shrugged, closing the door. She knew that Ryan had soccer practice and, on impulse, decided to watch. Maybe she could even give him a ride home.

She walked out to the field where the boys were working out. Marissa spotted Ryan bouncing a soccer ball on his knee. He was really good. He looked up and saw her, so Marissa waved. But Ryan didn't wave back. He just scowled and looked down, the soccer ball careening off his knee.

What was that about? Marissa wondered. Well, she was sure she'd find out on the ride home.

Look at her, acting like nothing has happened, like she's not back together with that asshole Luke, Ryan thought, unable to keep his eyes away from her even though he suspected that she was just leading him on, he thought. No matter how good she looked, it didn't change a single thing.

And speak of the jerk . . . Luke was running out onto the field, high-fiving all his jock buddies. Ryan's shoulders slurnped.

"Sorry, Coach, I had to tape up my ankle," Luke said.

"No problem. Let's see a scrimmage. Blues against reds." The coach tossed Luke a ball, and he jogged down the field.

Ryan glanced down at his own shirt. Blue. Luke was wearing red, and in Ryan's eyes, it was like waving a flag in front of a bull.

Ryan took off down the field, chasing Luke, who was easing the ball toward the goal. He dropped his head, sprinting, his cleats tearing up the field, determined not to let Luke have the satisfaction of beating him here, too.

Luke drew up alongside the goal, pulled up to kick the ball dead in, and — *WHAM!* Ryan slid in behind him, tackling him to the ground.

Ryan jumped up, his fists balled, ready to finish this fight. But Luke wasn't moving, and the coach was racing toward them, his whistle a steady stream.

"Hey. C'mon," Ryan said, surprised at the feeling of shame settling over him. He'd really hurt Luke. But wasn't that the whole point? He'd *wanted* to hurt him. So why was he feeling so guilty about it now?

He held out his hand to Luke to help him up. But before Luke could take it, the coach bustled over, pulling Luke up on his own.

"What's the matter with you, Atwood?" he demanded. "That was way too hard."

"It was a clean tackle," Ryan muttered, looking anywhere but at Luke.

"Maybe for the championship game. Not for the first day of practice. You just cost us our star player. You're sidelined."

As some of Luke's buddies helped their limping friend back to the locker room, Ryan slouched over to the bleachers and slumped down. Goddamn it. Why couldn't he ever win? He looked up, unaware of the accusing stares of the other kids. The only person he could see was Marissa, and she did not look happy.

By the time school ended and Ryan made it out to the student parking lot, Marissa's car was the only one left. He paused a few feet away, and Marissa rolled down her window.

"What the hell was that?" she asked.

"What?"

"You attacked him!"

"It's a game. You know all about games, don't you?" Ryan said, venom in his voice.

"What's that supposed to mean?" Marissa asked, genuinely confused.

"I saw you!" Ryan said, her innocent act only fueling his anger. "I saw you and Luke talking. I heard everything."

"Are you spying on me?" Two bright spots of pink appeared on Marissa's cheeks.

"I guess it's the only way I'll ever find out the truth," Ryan shot back.

"What happened was between me and Luke. It has nothing to do with you."

"Well, let's keep it that way," Ryan said, regretting the words even as he was speaking them. "You don't need to have anything to do with me, either. I'm walking home."

"Damn right you are," Marissa said, throwing the car into drive and squealing out of the parking lot.

Ryan watched her go, furious. At her? Or at himself? He could figure it out on the long walk home.

9

Here is what Marissa did before the school carnival benefit: chose an outfit, got a mani/pedi, took a shower, washed her hair, put on the outfit, took it off and chose a different outfit, put that one on, did her makeup, did her hair, thought about calling Ryan, picked up the phone, put it down, changed back into the first outfit, hunted for her car keys, found them, and went to pick up Summer.

Here is what Ryan did before the carnival: told Seth he wasn't going.

"You have to go!" Seth said. "Marissa and Summer are expecting us."

"Summer's not expecting you," Ryan said, amused.

Seth rolled his eyes. "But Marissa's going to be waiting for you, and since she'll be with Summer and since I love Summer, you have to go!"

"I don't think Marissa wants to see me," Ryan said.

Seth blew out an exasperated breath. "Look, do you want to be with Marissa?"

"Of course."

"So apologize."

"But she lied to me about Luke," Ryan said defensively.

Seth held up his hands, backing away. "I'm not saying you are in the wrong. I'm saying you should apologize *anyway*. If that's what it'll take to get her back."

"Maybe you're right," Ryan said, and Seth grinned.

"Great! Now go put on your shoes — Summer is expecting me!"

The carnival was truly the best charity event of the year. It was the one event where it was actually fun to help raise money for Harbor. You didn't have to dress up, it was held outside, and best of all?

"Skeeball." Seth handed the booth worker a strand of tickets and accepted three more balls. "I am a master at skeeball."

He gave Anna a cocky grin and tossed the first ball. "Score!"

"Not too shabby," she answered, and Seth cocked an eyebrow.

"You think you can do better?"

"Better than the amazing Cohen? Impossible," she answered, grabbing a ball and lining up the shot.

Bull's-eye.

"I am . . . humbled," Seth said, and handed her the winning tickets. "You deserve a really big" —

he scanned the pitiful selection of prizes hanging behind the booth — "a sock monkey . . ."

"Thank you," she said, smiling as the worker handed the stuffed toy to her. "You should keep this, to remember me."

"How could I ever forget you?" Seth asked. He flung his arm across her shoulders.

Anna grinned and slipped her arm around his waist. Finally! But when Ryan walked up to them, Seth pulled his arm back.

"Have you seen Marissa?" Ryan asked. Seth shook his head. "No, man, and I haven't seen Summer, either."

"Damn. I really need to talk to her."

"I saw her earlier over by the rides," Anna said. "Why don't you look for her there."

"Yeah, thanks," Ryan said. He took off, and Seth started after him. But when he noticed Anna wasn't following, he stopped.

"Summer might be there, too," he said, and looked surprised at Anna's scowl. "What?"

Anna blew out a frustrated breath. "Nothing. Just come on." She stalked after Ryan, leaving Seth behind to wonder what girls were thinking.

In his rush to find Marissa, Ryan, meanwhile, was hurrying across the fairground so quickly that he banged into someone.

"Watch where you're going," said the person in annoyance. "Sorry" was halfway out of Ryan's mouth before he realized the person he had just bumped into was Luke.

"Oh," Ryan said, and the two boys stared at each other for a long minute.

Luke opened his mouth, but before he could say anything, Ryan jumped in. "Look. I'm sorry. About yesterday."

Luke looked past Ryan, to where Marissa was about to get on the Ferris wheel. Ryan saw her, too, and his face twitched with a question he was unwilling to ask.

"I think I get it," Luke said quietly, and for the briefest instant there was a flicker of something between them that said they might never be friends, but at least they understood each other.

Luke's buddies called to him to join them, and before he even turned away, Ryan was streaking toward Marissa.

Summer was climbing into the cart of the Ferris wheel after Marissa, when Ryan stopped her. "You mind?" he asked, clambering inside.

"Not getting involved," Summer said, stepping aside to let Ryan by.

"What do you think you're doing?" Marissa asked angrily, but it was too late. The operator lowered the bar and the car rose slowly into the air.

"I want to talk to you — oh god!" Ryan gulped as the cart lurched. He stared straight ahead, not daring to look down, and Marissa noticed that his knuckles were clutching the safety bar so hard they were white.

"What's wrong?" Marissa asked, forgetting her

anger at the sight of big tough Ryan in so much distress.

"I'm not so good with heights," he said.

"Then why did you follow me on here?"

"I needed to tell you that I'm sorry for saying those things to you yester — whoa! What's happening?!" Ryan finished in a panic as the wheel clanked to a halt.

Marissa leaned over the side of the cart and peered at the operator on the ground far below. "We're stopped," she said easily. Now that Ryan had apologized, she didn't mind a little delay. In fact, sitting there close to Ryan, she didn't mind if the wheel stayed still all night.

On the ground, Seth was staring in shock at Anna, who had just handed the operator a folded twenty. "Keep 'em up there for a few minutes," she told him. "Let them work it out."

"You are the master," Seth said, admiration ready in his voice.

Anna looked at him. It was so easy to fix other people's relationships. Time to do a little something for her own.

"So. Cohen. There's something I want to tell you."

"Excellent. What?" Seth asked.

"This," Anna said, reaching her arms up around his neck. She got up on tiptoe, pulling his face to hers, and before she had time to think or get scared or change her mind, she kissed him.

It took Seth only a second of confusion to start kissing her back. This was his fourth kiss ever. The first happened when he was thirteen, at the Bat Mitzvah of a distant cousin. That one didn't count because it was a relative. Seth's second kiss was with a girl in his sailing class. She was moving to a different town the next day with her family, and at her going-away party, she pulled Seth into the bushes behind the boathouse and kissed him. Seth later found out that she had kissed every single boy there, so clearly that kiss didn't count, either. And then there was the kiss Summer had given him at Casino Night . . .but that was just because she was winning. Which made this . . . his first real kiss? It felt like it — Anna's lips were about the softest thing he had ever felt, and she even made a little purring noise in the back of her throat that made him want to crush her against him and never let her go.

But . . . when they finally did separate, before he could kiss her again, they looked over to see Summer staring at them, openmouthed and stricken. Seth glanced at Anna and saw a little smile curling across her lips, and realized that maybe that kiss was just a part of Anna's plan to help him win Summer. And if it was, he probably shouldn't kiss her again. Even though he really wanted to. Even though Summer was walking away.

Fifty feet in the air, Ryan was too busy trying not to completely freak out to think about anything but plummeting to his death. Although Marissa's leg was pressed up against his, and he could feel her warmth through the fabric of her jeans.

"Are you okay?" she asked him, putting her hand on his. He took a deep breath, trying to turn enough in the seat to face her without jostling the cart any more than absolutely necessary.

"Look. I don't talk a lot . . . about stuff," he started, ". . . and I don't really trust people. But . . . I do trust you. And I want to make this work. No matter what."

Marissa smiled, moved. "Ryan —" and then she was kissing him, her hands reaching around him, his hands tangling in her hair.

She pressed against him, her mouth sealing his mouth, her tongue lightly teasing his, and Ryan groaned, forgetting the heights and his fear and the vulnerability of his confession. His whole world became the heat of her breath, the softness of her skin, the feel of her arms pulling him tight. He kissed her like her lips were the way to salvation, and when the operator started the motor again and the wheel began to move, Ryan wasn't scared. In fact, he didn't even notice.

10

Once they started kissing, it was hard for Ryan and Marissa to stop. When they were together, Marissa could forget about the problems her family was having, and Ryan was able to set aside his worries over the fact that after six weeks at Harbor, he was no closer to catching up to the other students than he had been at the beginning of the school year.

English, especially, was proving to be his sticking point. He'd read the books they were assigned and understood them, but when the teacher asked questions about them, it was like he had read an entirely different book from the rest of the class. And instead of taking tests where you could write down what you thought the fish in *The Old Man and the Sea* symbolized, the teacher based her class grades on what she called "open discussion," where you were supposed to say what you thought in front of the entire class . . . which Ryan just wasn't going to do. Period.

So he was pretty much dreading getting his report card in a couple of weeks. He knew the news wouldn't be good, and he wasn't sure what Kirsten and Sandy would have to say about that. Sandy was always encouraging, telling Ryan he knew he was smart and able to do the work, and Ryan really didn't want to disappoint him. Especially since he knew Seth was making straight A's without even trying.

But when he was with Marissa, he could forget about school. To tell the truth, when he had Marissa in his arms, he couldn't have remembered school even if he wanted to. She drove everything else out of his head, leaving nothing but desire. He wanted her more than he had ever wanted another girl, but at the same time, he felt protective of her, like it was up to him to keep her safe and make sure no one ever made her sad again. He would have been surprised if he knew it, but Marissa was thinking the exact same thing about him, and because of this, without discussing it at all, they decided to take it slow. Like, Ice Age slow. Neither of them wanted to move too fast and scare the other one off, so they limited themselves to just kissing.

In the pool house, in her car, before school, late at night, any second they could steal to be to-gether they were, but they always made sure when their kissing turned urgent, when they suddenly caught themselves sweating and breathless, pressed together so hard it seemed like they would melt into each other, they always pulled away. Even if they thought they'd probably die if they didn't have sex right that second, they always managed to resist.

"But you have, right? Before? Had sex, I mean?" Seth asked Ryan. The two boys were walking across the quad to their next class, and Ryan had just let drop that he and Marissa hadn't done it yet.

Ryan glanced at Seth, who was looking at him with such eager curiosity that he had to laugh. "Sure," he said, and Seth's eyes lit up.

"I knew it! I mean, that's what I thought. I just didn't want to jump to conclusions, since my experience is . . . limited." He paused, looking to Ryan for details. Ryan didn't volunteer any. So:

"And?"

Another sideways glance from Ryan. "And what?"

"Was it awesome?"

"Which time?" Ryan asked, keeping a perfectly straight face, and Seth stopped dead in his tracks.

"How many times were there?"

"Same girl," Ryan asked, amused as hell at Seth's reaction, "or different girls?"

Now Seth actually staggered backward, clutching at his chest with one hand. "There were different girls? How many?"

Ryan started counting them up on his fingers. When he got to his second hand, Seth shook his head, staggering toward a nearby bench. "Okay, I'm gonna need to sit down."

Across the quad, Summer and Marissa were also discussing the state of things.

"I don't want to move too fast," Marissa said, "I don't want to do anything to ruin it."

"Coop, he's a *guy*. It's impossible to move too fast."

"Well, maybe I don't want to move too fast for me. Sex is a big deal. I don't know if I'm ready yet."

"But Luke already took care of the hard part," Summer said thoughtlessly, then stopped. She put her hand on her friend's arm. "Sorry."

"Yeah, and look how well that worked out. I definitely don't want a repeat of that with Ryan. Besides, we're still getting to know each other."

"But once you get to know him, you'll do it?" Summer asked, grinning.

Marissa's grin managed to be even wider than Summer's. "Definitely."

Marissa stopped by her dad's apartment that afternoon on her way to Ryan's. She wanted to drop off her books and change into the new pink shirt she'd bought over the weekend. But when she unlocked the door and went inside, she was shocked to find her mother sitting on the couch.

"Hi, sweetie," Julie said with a tentative smile. But Marissa wasn't ready to make nice with her just yet.

"What are you doing here?" she asked coldly.

"Your mom was in the area and thought she'd stop by," Jimmy answered for her, coming in from the kitchen. He was carrying two glasses of iced tea and handed one to Julie, offering the other to Marissa.

She shook her head, still glaring at her mother.

"Well, you've stopped, so . . ." she said, and Julie sighed, taking a second to steel herself before she got down to the reason for her visit.

"Guess what? I'm throwing a party," she said brightly. She glanced at Jimmy, who seemed open to hearing more, then at Marissa, who did not. She forged ahead anyway. "It's a benefit for the Children's Hospital this Saturday. They're trying to build a new wing." She paused, then — "I'd love it if you would be there. Your father has already agreed."

"No. No way," Marissa said, dismayed. She couldn't believe her father had betrayed her like that. How could he want to spend more time with Julie after the way she'd treated them?

But Julie kept talking, her voice steady. "This party is a chance for us to show the community that we're still a family. That we still belong. No matter what happened with your father's business" — here she threw a sidelong look at Jimmy, who smiled innocently and sipped his tea — "we need to let Newport know that the Cooper family is still here."

Marissa didn't answer, and Julie's smile faltered. "Please, sweetie. This is important to me."

"Why should I care about helping you?" Marissa asked, a little surprised herself at the anger in her voice.

"I am so sorry for the way I handled things when you were in the hospital," Julie said. "I was scared. Everything I cared about was falling apart, and I blamed everybody but myself. Trying to send you away was wrong. And now all I want is for us to feel like a family again." Julie sniffed, looking at her lap as she quickly blotted some tears from her eyes.

Jimmy moved closer to the couch, his expression a mixture of love, concern, doubt. Julie reached for his hand and he took it. She stretched her other hand out to Marissa, who hesitated.

"I know it's going to take time. But can we try?"

And before she knew what she was doing, Marissa took her mother's hand and was pulled into her parents' embrace.

11

Ryan was lying on his bed in the pool house, avoiding homework with one of Seth's Fantastic Four comics, when there was a knock at the door: two short, two long, Marissa's special code. Ryan shoved the comic under his pillow and sat up, running a hand through his hair as Marissa came in.

"Hey," he said, pulling her down next to him. He wrapped his arms around her in a tight hug, amazed as always that she was his and he could hold her as long as he wanted. "I was wondering what happened to you."

"I just talked to my mom," Marissa said, curling up against Ryan's shoulder. She picked up his hand in both of hers and lightly traced her finger across his palm, the life line, the love line.

"You okay?" he asked in a grim voice, anticipating her bad mood, but when she tilted her face up to his, her expression was happier than he'd seen it in a long time.

"She apologized to me! For how she's been.

And I think she means it. I think she's really changed."

"That's incredible," Ryan said, smiling at her excitement.

"I'm glad you think so," Marissa said, concentrating hard on reading his palm, "because she wants us to come to her benefit this Saturday."

Ryan grimaced. "Your mom . . . hates me. Maybe I shouldn't go, give you guys some time together."

"She doesn't hate you," Marissa said, "and this will give her a chance to see that for herself. Besides, you have to come."

"Oh yeah? Why?"

"It's on Seth's grandfather's yacht."

"Is that the only reason?"

Marissa shook her head. "No. There's also this —" She reached her arms up around his neck and pulled his mouth down to hers.

And they were kissing again.

Inside the house, Anna was trouncing Seth at Jenga. "I could be a surgeon," she said, holding her hand out so Seth could see how steady it was. "And I'll just sliiiiiide this piece out. . . ." Anna captured a particularly difficult middle piece, and Seth groaned, throwing his hands up in the air.

"One day, when you're least expecting it — watch out!" he said, trying to duplicate her moves on a Jenga block, and sighing as the entire pile came crashing down.

"How about Saturday?" Anna said. "We can

rent old Molly Ringwald movies and get pizza and have an all-night tournament."

"Can't on Saturday," Seth said. "I have to go to this charity thing on my grandpa's yacht."

"Oh. Some other time, then," Anna said, picking at a loose thread on one of the couch cushions she was leaning against. She and Seth had never discussed their kiss, and things had kept on as normal. But that was precisely the problem — Anna didn't want things to stay the same with Seth, and she wasn't sure what else she could do to make him realize that, at least not while he still spent every waking hour talking about stupid Summer.

"Actually," Seth continued, stacking the Jenga blocks back up for a rematch, "how do you feel about Newport social events?"

"I hate them," Anna answered, feeling her heart start to beat a little faster.

"Me, too," Seth said. "So, what do you say you come to one with me? We'll hang out and quietly mock people."

"It's a date," Anna said, and meant it.

Ryan and Marissa lay on his bed, completely tangled up in each other. Ryan moved his mouth from Marissa's lips to her neck, kissing his way down to the soft curve of her shoulder.

Marissa moaned and slid her hands up under the back of his shirt, digging her fingers into his warm skin.

Now it was Ryan's turn to moan, and he moved

back to her mouth, the friction of their bodies colliding against each other almost too much for him to bear.

Almost . . . but not quite. It was anguish to pull away from her, but he did, shifting his body off hers as Marissa slid out from underneath him, trying not to let him see just how breathless he actually made her.

"I should go," she said, reaching for her sandals. She pulled them on, then stood up and smiled at him. "See you tomorrow?"

"Definitely," Ryan said. He started to get up, but Marissa knew if he touched her one more time she would lose all self-control and attack him right there, so she gave a little wave and slipped out the door before he could reach her.

Ryan smiled and stretched lazily. Forget about getting any work done tonight. He might as well go into the house and see what Seth was up to, if he wanted to play some video games or something.

He could hear Marissa's car drive off, and he smiled again. He walked out by the pool and looked out after the fading lights of her car. It was a gorgeous night, warm and clear, and the sky was full of stars. Ryan looked up at them to make a wish, then realized he couldn't think of anything he needed to wish for — for the first time in his life, he actually felt completely content.

But almost before the thought *I'm happy* could form itself in his head, a sleek Lexus SUV pulled into the driveway of Julie Cooper's house next door. As Ryan watched, Julie got out, followed by Seth's grandfather, Caleb. Caleb captured Julie around the waist and pulled her to him in a long, passionate kiss.

Surprised, Ryan ducked out of sight. But the movement caught Julie's eye over Caleb's shoulder. She and Ryan locked gazes, and Ryan felt a sinking feeling as he realized what this meant for Marissa's fantasies of her family going back to normal.

And as Julie pulled Caleb inside her house and shut the door behind them, Ryan had to wonder just what this meant for him, too.

12

Ryan managed to avoid mentioning what he'd seen to Marissa all week but had serious worries about what would happen when he was face-to-face with Julie Cooper on Saturday night. He tried a couple of times to bring up his skipping the party, but Marissa was so wrapped up in the thought of her parents together and happy again that she missed all his hints.

And the next thing he knew, Saturday had rolled around and Marissa was hanging out in the pool house, waiting for him to finish getting dressed. She leafed through the copy of *Kavalier and Clay* that Seth kept slipping into Ryan's stack of required reading, one finger absentmindedly twirling a strand of hair into knots.

"Really, she's like a different person," she told Ryan, who was hunting in vain for the pair of hand-me-down dress shoes that Sandy had given him. "Who knows, if everything goes all right tonight with my parents, then maybe I'll be living next door to you again." She looked so hopeful that Ryan couldn't think of a single answer that wouldn't crush her, so he just smiled and held up a pair of boots.

"Can I get away with these?"

Marissa laughed and shook her head, and Ryan vowed to do whatever it took to keep the sadness out of her expression.

Seth, meanwhile, had quite a shock when he opened the front door to find Anna looking better than he'd ever seen her. Maybe even better than Summer, if that was possible.

"Anna — wow, you . . . great dress," he trailed off, looking her up and down.

Anna smiled and moved past him to the glass doorway to the pool, deliberately letting her body brush against his. "You ever use the hot tub?"

Seth gulped, checking out the back view — every bit as good as the front one. "Well, I usually just hang in the grotto."

Anna laughed, and Seth finally recognized the old Anna in her face. And if anything? It made him like her even more.

Ryan and Marissa came walking in from the pool house and said hi. "Everybody ready?" Marissa asked the group.

"You bet. Tonight should be fun," Anna said, slipping her arm through Seth's.

"There's going to be a raffle. And the only thing

more fun than a raffle is . . . well, anything, really," Seth said.

The gang all laughed and rolled their eyes, and with that they were out the door and on their way to Julie Cooper's party.

13

When Julie Cooper said the benefit would be spectacular, she wasn't kidding: everybody in black tie, waiters passing enormous trays of delectable hors d'oeuvres, music filling the air, and lights glinting off the water around Caleb's gigantic luxury yacht.

Julie and Jimmy were standing at the entrance to the main deck together, greeting the guests as they filed aboard. When Marissa saw them, her eyes lit up, and she gave her mom a kiss on the cheek.

"Hey! You made it!" Julie said happily. Watching the tableau, all Ryan could feel was a surge of anger, knowing that Julie was going to break Marissa's heart all over again. Julie could see the rage flitting across Ryan's features, because when she finally let Marissa go, she took his arm chummily and led him a few steps away, out of hearing distance from the rest of the guests.

"I know you and I haven't always seen eye to eye," she told him, her voice perfectly convivial, "but I'm hoping this party will be a chance for us to start fresh. All of us."

"You mean you and Caleb Nichol?" Ryan asked, extricating his arm from her grasp.

Julie sighed, her features hardening. "You don't know anything about it."

"I know Marissa thinks this party is the first step in you getting back together with her dad," Ryan said angrily. "You might be okay with lying to her, but I'm not."

"It's none of your business, Ryan," she said. "This is my life. My daughter."

"She's my girlfriend. That makes it my business," he said, and stalked away, leaving her shooting daggers into his retreating back.

Ryan spotted Marissa standing by the bar with Summer, sipping martinis and looking across the deck to where Seth and Anna were leaning against the railing, their heads close together, utterly absorbed in what the other had to say.

"What is Seth Cohen doing with Tinkerbell? She's such a little scammer," Summer said disgustedly.

"Anna's cool," Marissa said, somehow managing to feel disloyal to both girls.

Summer turned on her, outraged. "Are you kidding? Have you seen the way she looks at him?"

"No, but clearly you have," Ryan said, coming up behind them and slipping his arms around Marissa's waist. Marissa giggled and leaned back against his chest, craning her neck up to kiss him, and Summer transferred her disgust onto them.

"Shut up."

"It's totally obvious," Marissa said, teasing. "You like Seth Cohen."

"I do not like Seth Cohen. I can't like Seth Cohen," Summer protested.

"Too bad. 'Cause he likes you," Marissa said, finishing her martini in one gulp and grabbing another off a passing tray as Ryan dragged her away.

Summer watched them go, but she wasn't thinking about the fact that they had left her alone. The only thought in her mind? *Oh my god. I like Seth Cohen.*

Ryan pulled Marissa over to a stairway, and together they climbed up onto a higher deck. No one else was up there, and if it weren't for the sounds from the crowd below, they could almost pretend to be completely alone, with nothing but the sea and the moon for company.

"It's so beautiful here," Marissa said, looking out over the water.

"You're beautiful," Ryan answered, nuzzling her neck.

But Marissa was too fueled by the sight of her parents getting along to totally lose herself in the moment.

"You know what? If my dad can find a job soon, I think we might move back in. And then I could sneak over whenever I wanted."

Ryan's heart sank. He didn't want to spoil the evening, but he also couldn't keep this secret from her any longer. So he just shrugged. "Parents are weird. I wouldn't count on anything."

Marissa turned to face him, annoyance clear on her face. "Why are you trying to ruin this for me?"

"I'm not —"

"Why can't you just be happy for me? My parents are probably going to get back together."

"No, they won't," Ryan said softly, staring down at the washed wooden boards of the deck.

"What are you saying?" Marissa asked, her voice rising in pitch.

Damn it. Ryan had to tell her. "Your mom is seeing Caleb Nichol."

"What? What are you talking about?"

"I saw them," Ryan said, wanting to hold her but not sure if she would stand for being touched right now. "I saw them in front of your house. Together."

Marissa stared at him for a second without moving, without saying anything, without even breathing.

"I'm sorry," Ryan said softly.

But without a word, Marissa turned on her heel and set off back down the stairs to the main deck.

Bracing himself for whatever happened next, Ryan followed her.

Seth and Anna were still leaning against the railing of the main deck, mocking people according to their plan.

"My god," Anna said as a group of X-ray-thin women teetered past. "Pittsburgh does not have people like this."

Seth gave her a little nudge with his shoulder. "You must really hate Newport."

"I did," Anna said, "at first. But now? It's growing on me."

Seth looked at her and in an instant, everything became clear. Anna liked him. Really liked him. The way he liked Summer. And if he wanted to, all he'd have to do was lean forward. Lean forward and kiss her, and his whole life would get really good. Only — it would be with Anna, not Summer, and Seth wasn't sure what he thought about that.

Probably it would be completely fantastic, but then again . . . he'd liked Summer forever. Named his boat after her. Burned a CD of songs all containing the word *summer*. Spent every night of his life picturing Summer's face as he fell asleep. Could he really just replace it all with Anna? He couldn't even think of any songs with the name Anna in them.

After a minute, Seth realized that Anna had stopped being ready to be kissed and was actually looking a little pissed. Well, at least that bought him some time.

"Are you thirsty?" he asked, trying not to notice the hurt and disappointment in her eyes. "'Cause I'll go get us some drinks or something . . . okay. Good." And he turned and ran, not daring to look back.

* * *

Seth downed a Mountain Dew at the downstairs bar, not caring that everyone around him was getting drunk. He needed to keep his wits about him — god only knew what else Anna had in store for him tonight. He ordered a couple more for himself and Anna, then started back along the corridor of staterooms toward the main deck.

But when one of the stateroom doors opened and Summer's arm shot out and grabbed him, he was so surprised he spilled one of the Mountain Dews all down his shirtfront.

"Hey! Be careful," he said, more surprised than mad, but Summer wasn't listening. She pulled him into the room, shoved him up against the wall, and stuck her tongue in his mouth.

Seth dropped the other glass of Mountain Dew.

Summer kissed Seth as passionately as she knew how, grinding her body up against his as she devoured him with her mouth. Seth kissed her back, frantically trying to record every second of the kiss in his brain so when he woke up or snapped out of this delusion, he would remember just how soul-stirring it actually was.

Seth honestly couldn't tell if the kiss went on for seconds or hours, but finally Summer wrenched herself away, a horrified look on her face. "Oh god, no," she said, truly distressed.

"What's going on here?" Seth demanded. "What's happening?"

"I like Seth Cohen," Summer said, disbelievingly.

"What?" Seth asked. But instead of answering him, Summer raced out the door, and disappeared down the corridor.

"What?" Seth asked again, and in a daze, wandered back toward the main deck, more confused than he could ever have imagined.

Julie Cooper, meanwhile, had set up a microphone on the main deck and was getting ready to address her guests. "Hi," she said into the mic, "Thank you all for coming tonight. So far, through your contributions, we've raised almost two hundred thousand dollars for the Children's Hospital."

The crowd applauded and Julie smiled. Marissa stood on the edge of the crowd, Ryan at her side. She wasn't looking at her mom, though. She was staring holes into Caleb, who was following Julie's every move with a self-satisfied smirk on his face.

"It's time for the raffle," Julie continued. "We're giving away a romantic week for two in Hawaii. I'd like to ask my beautiful daughter Marissa to do the honors. Come join me, sweetie."

Marissa looked at Ryan. "Ready for this?"

"Why don't we just go?" Ryan begged, but Marissa was already making her way to the microphone, an evil smirk playing across her features.

Ryan watched helplessly as Marissa took the microphone from her mom.

"Thanks. Can I get another round of applause for my mom?"

The crowd happily obliged, and Julie beamed at her daughter.

"And for Caleb Nichol?" The crowd's clapping continued, but Julie's face lost some of its enthusiasm. "After all their work on behalf of the Children's Hospital, if anybody deserves a romantic getaway, it's the two of them."

Now the applause was more tentative, and Julie moved to take the microphone back, but Marissa wasn't going to be stopped.

"Aren't they just the perfect couple?" she continued, her voice as bright as she could make it. "They've been keeping their romance a secret, but tonight? The secret's out. Congratulations, guys," she said, and dropped the microphone to the floor.

The squealing feedback of the sound system was drowned out by the buzz of the gossip-hungry crowd. Marissa stormed off the stage, Ryan tagging at her heels. Julie stood frozen in the middle of the room, all eyes on her, looking for an escape route from Jimmy who was heading toward her, obviously burning with questions that she had no interest in answering.

And into the middle of all this mayhem wandered Seth. He walked up to Anna, unable to meet her eyes. But Anna was too busy drinking in this newest bit of Newport scandal to notice.

"You'll never believe what you missed," she said.

Maybe not, but Seth had had enough excitement for one night. All he wanted to do was crawl into bed and figure things out. "You ready to go?" he asked Anna.

She smiled and leaned against him, wrapping one arm around his waist. "Let's go," she answered.

Marissa and Ryan were also beating a hasty retreat. They'd gotten as far as the parking lot when Julie caught up with them.

"What the hell was that?" she demanded.

"You lied to me," Marissa shouted, her fury boiling over. "You said you wanted us to be a family again."

"I do!" Julie insisted. "This whole party was to show you that if you moved back home, we could be a family again."

"What about Dad?" Marissa asked, hating the fact that she was starting to cry.

"I will always love your father," Julie said calmly. "But because of what he's done, we have no future together."

"Then neither do we," Marissa said. She turned away from her mother, taking hold of Ryan's sleeve and dragging him with her toward the car.

Ryan looked back at Julie, who was watching her daughter walk away from her again, and for the first time since he'd met her, felt nothing for her but pity.

"Let's go," Marissa said to him, and Ryan turned his back on Julie Cooper, leaving her standing alone amidst the ruins of her party.

14

Report cards came out a couple weeks later, and as Ryan had feared, the news was not good. If anything, since Marissa had officially severed all communication with her mother, Ryan had fallen even further behind. He couldn't let Marissa down in her time of need, but at the same time, if things didn't change, public school was looking more and more likely.

"Maybe we should get you a tutor," Kirsten suggested. She put a plate of takeout Thai food down in front of him and let her hand rest on his shoulder for a minute.

"I don't know if that would do any good," Ryan said. He stared down at the food — he was too depressed to eat.

"Well, maybe Seth can help you," Sandy suggested, "and for that matter, I'm no slouch in the sciences myself."

"Maybe," Ryan said. He dejectedly stuffed half a spring roll into his mouth, then mumbled through it. "What I really need is a couple weeks with nothing else to do, so I can get caught up to the rest of the class."

"Well, you've got that," Kirsten said. "Or one week, at least." He looked at her blankly. "Thanks-giving, silly. You'll have eight days to really get on top of things."

"Huh," Ryan said, shoveling another mouthful of pad thai in before he'd finished chewing the first. "I bet if I stayed in and studied the whole time, I could get through some of this."

"There you go," Sandy said. He spooned some food onto his own plate and settled down at the table across from Ryan.

"Yeah, and Marissa is going up to Berkeley with her dad that Friday, so I'll be able to really concen-trate on my work." Ryan finally felt his appetite coming back, although when he looked down at his plate, half the food was gone. Kirsten passed him the takeout container.

"How are things going with Marissa?" she asked him in a very parental-sounding voice.

"She's still not talking to her mom, but she's supposed to see her for Thanksgiving dinner, so I don't know," Ryan said.

"I meant" — Kirsten glanced at Sandy, who made a self-conscious "go on" gesture with his hand — "how are things going with *you* and Marissa?"

"Oh," Ryan said. What exactly were they trying to ask him? "Good, I mean, great. No complaints."

"What Kirsten is trying to ask you," Sandy said,

also not sounding anything like himself, "is if you have any questions, or if you and Marissa are, well —"

"— being careful," Kirsten finished. The Cohens both stared down at the tabletop, and Ryan grinned at how uncomfortable they seemed.

"Yeah."

"Yeah?" Sandy asked. "What's yeah?"

"Yeah, things are good; yeah, we're being careful; no, you don't need to worry."

"It's just . . ." Kirsten started, and both men looked at her. "We've never had to have this talk with Seth."

"Well, it's probably a good thing that you practiced on me first," Ryan said, and helped himself to the last of the spring rolls as Kirsten and Sandy stared at him, then each other.

Wednesday afternoon, Ryan lugged all his books home from school, even ones he didn't have assigned work in. He plopped them all down on the dining table, but Kirsten came in and stopped him before he could get too comfortable.

"Maybe you should get yourself set up in the kitchen so you won't have to clear everything away for dinner tomorrow."

"We're eating in the dining room?" Ryan asked, and Seth, walking in, answered him.

"Yes, it's a tradition, along with Dad setting the table and Mom ordering all the food in from the caterers."

"You aren't going to give the turkey a shot?" Ryan teased Kirsten, and Seth stared at him, aghast.

"Please don't even joke about that. Thanksgiving is one of my very favorite holidays; Mom cooking would ruin everything."

"I could cook," Kirsten said sharply, but Seth put a patronizing arm around her and ushered her toward the door.

"Mom. Come on. You know we love the way you order catering. Isn't that enough?"

Kirsten gave him a look. "Help Ryan move his books to the kitchen."

Ryan got started on his work right away, and by the time he was ready to call it a night, he'd gotten most of the way through his bio homework, and with Sandy's help, was even pretty solid on understanding the respiratory system.

"You should be studying the *digestive* system," Seth told him, rummaging through the fridge for a midnight snack.

"You're eating again?" Ryan asked him, slamming his book shut and taking a slice of the cold pizza Seth had scrounged up.

"I'm preparing my stomach for tomorrow," Seth told him. "The more I stretch it out now, the more food I can fit into it tomorrow."

"On that note . . ." Ryan said, starting out of the kitchen.

"Hey, want to play some *Deimos Rising* before

you go to bed?" Seth asked, but Ryan shook his head.

"Nope. Nothing but studying this week, so I'm going to go get started on *Gatsby* for English."

The next morning, Ryan was back at the kitchen table before any of the Cohens woke up. He pulled out his Spanish vocabulary sheets and got down to work, feeling pretty damn satisfied with himself for how much he'd already accomplished. By the time the Cohens had gotten out of bed and were pouring their coffee, Ryan was feeling for the first time that he might actually be able to handle the workload at Harbor. As long as nothing happened to interrupt his studying —

Of course the phone chose to ring at that exact second, and by the look on Kirsten's face as she handed the receiver to him, Ryan's hopes for a quiet weekend of work deserted him.

"It's for you, Ryan," Kirsten said. "It's your brother."

Aware of all the eyes of the Cohens on him, Ryan took the phone and walked toward the door. "I'm gonna take it outside," he said quietly, and slid the glass door shut behind him.

The Cohens all looked at one another.

"This feels weird, right?" Seth asked his parents. They nodded.

"It's strange," Kirsten said. "I've gotten so used to Ryan being a part of our family that I forgot he has one of his own."

Outside, Ryan held the phone to his ear with a trembling hand. "Trey. How are you?"

"Hey, little man," Trey answered, his voice sounding tinny and far away. "Happy Thanksgiving."

"You, too," Ryan said. He thought he could hear the shouts and noise of the other inmates in the background, and it brought the awful memory of his own time in juvie rushing back. "So . . . what do you want?"

"What, I can't call my little brother to say hi?" Trey asked, and when Ryan didn't answer, he sighed. "There is one thing —"

Ryan's heart sank. He knew it. He *knew* it. Trey wanted something that would be hard or dangerous or downright impossible for Ryan to do. But he was his brother, and Trey would make sure Ryan really felt the obligation, so he would be guilted into doing whatever it was.

A few minutes later, Ryan hung up the phone feeling oddly optimistic. Trey wanted to see him. Maybe this holiday would mark the beginning of a new stage in their relationship, maybe he and Trey could eventually be brothers. He walked back into the kitchen where the Cohens were waiting — but trying not to be obvious about it.

"How's Trey?" Sandy asked when Ryan came back in. The whole family was staring at him.

"He's okay. He wanted me to visit him. Um, do you think I could maybe borrow your car?"

"Absolutely," Kirsten said, digging her keys out

of her purse and handing them to him. "You go see him, and we'll wait to have dinner until you get back."

Seth started to protest, but the look Kirsten shot at him stopped the words in his throat. "We'd be happy to wait for you before we start eating," he said contritely.

"I'll be back soon," Ryan told them, and took one last look at his new family before he went back to face his old one.

Ryan was pulling out of the driveway when he saw Marissa waving to him from the porch of her mother's house. He pulled over and rolled down the window, and Marissa ran down to his car.

"Hi," she said, leaning in for a kiss.

Ryan happily gave it to her. "What are you doing here?"

"I'm supposed to have dinner with my mom and she's not even here. It's so typical." Marissa tossed her hair, then started over with a smile. "So, where are you off to?"

"I'm going to see my brother," Ryan said

"Well, why don't I come with you?" Marissa said, opening the passenger door and slipping into the seat next to him.

"I don't think so," Ryan said, but Marissa buckled her seat belt and crossed her arms.

"Why not? It'll be fun."

"It won't be fun," Ryan told her. "Marissa —"

Seth Cohen's always on the outside looking in at the O.C.

Seth goes from no girlfriend to two . . . can he pull it off?

Marissa and Ryan try to figure out where they stand.

The school year begins . . .

With Marissa, Ryan has to conquer several things, including his fear of . . . heights.

Valentine's Day surprise! Ryan's old girl-friend, Theresa, is working at the party.

Love may come and go in the O.C., but friendship is forever.

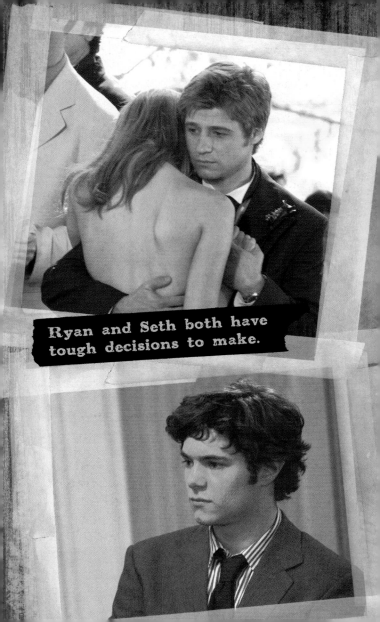

Ryan and Seth both have tough decisions to make.

"I'm going," she told him, "so you might as well start the car and drive."

So Ryan did.

The visit with Trey at the prison did not go well. He wasn't really interested in seeing Ryan, except that he needed a favor.

"I need you to pick up my car from Arturo's and drop it at Gattas's garage."

Christ, it was worse than he thought. Trey's car was stolen, for one thing, and god only knew what kind of lowlife Gattas was. But . . .

"Does this have to be today?" he asked. "'Cause I'm pretty busy —"

"What, eating turkey with your rich new friends?" Trey asked angrily. "They're gonna *kill me*, man, and you're sitting there eating goddamn Pillsbury rolls in the O.C. while I'm rotting away in here."

"Fine," Ryan said, resigned. "I'll pick up the car."

"Thanks, man," Trey said. "You're a good brother, you know that?"

"I'll let you know when I've dropped off the car," Ryan said.

On the drive to Chino, Ryan was silent. Marissa didn't try to get him to talk. She just looked out the window, seeing the run-down buildings and trash-filled streets of Ryan's old home with new eyes. She'd driven past on her way to Los

Angeles a bunch of times, but she never really stopped to think about the people who lived there. Ryan hadn't told her what sort of errand they needed to run, so she was surprised when he pulled down a side street and brought the car to a stop in front of a small, cheerful house.

"Is this where you used to live?" she asked tentatively, but Ryan shook his head.

"Friend of my brother," Ryan said, getting out of the door and slamming the door shut. Marissa followed him up to the porch, standing a little behind him as he rang the bell.

She wasn't sure what she was expecting, but it definitely wasn't the gorgeous, tough-looking, dark-haired teenage girl who opened the door and threw her arms around Ryan's neck.

"Ryan Atwood!" she exclaimed, hugging him tightly for a minute, then abruptly pulling away. "Where the hell have you been for the last five months?"

"Hey, Theresa," Ryan said, shifting his weight from one foot to the other.

Theresa stared at him for a minute, waiting for an answer to her question. When none came, she shifted her focus to Marissa. "Who are you?"

"I'm Marissa Cooper," she said, smiling and extending her hand to shake.

Theresa shook her head. "This is your *new* girlfriend?" she asked Ryan, her eyes still on Marissa. Ryan hung his head.

"Oh," said Marissa, the realization hitting her, "you two were . . . ?"

Theresa nodded. "I was the girl next door."

"So am I," Marissa said.

The two girls looked at Ryan, who ducked his head. "Arturo here?" he asked, and Theresa called over her shoulder for him.

"Hey," Arturo said, appearing a second later. "You come for the car?"

Ryan nodded.

"Come on," Arturo said, and the two boys disappeared around the back of the house.

Theresa gave Marissa a long, appraising look, then shrugged. "You might as well come in," she said, walking into the house. And with no other choice, Marissa followed.

15

Theresa went into the kitchen and picked up a paring knife and some potatoes. Her Thanksgiving dinner preparations were well under way, and a little thing like Ryan showing up out of the blue wasn't going to throw her.

Marissa hovered by the stove uncertainly. "Can I help with anything?" she asked, but Theresa shook her head.

"That's okay. I wouldn't want you to get your hands dirty," she said, deftly sweeping the peels into the garbage.

"I don't mind," Marissa said lamely and, when Theresa didn't bother to answer her, gave up. God, she hated her already. She was exactly the type of girl Marissa would have imagined for Ryan, sexy and aggressive and scarily self-confident . . . the exact opposite of herself. Theresa seemed like nothing could ever upset her, like no matter what happened, she could take care of herself.

But if that was the case, Marissa wondered, why

was she unable to look Marissa in the eye? After all, Ryan chose *her*, and no matter how tough Theresa acted, it was pretty apparent that she missed him. Feeling a little better about the situation, Marissa relaxed, checking out the photographs stuck to the refrigerator door.

"Oh my god, is this Ryan?" she asked. The picture showed a younger Ryan and Theresa dressed up in costume, beaming at the camera, their arms around each other. Ryan had on floppy ears and a blacked-out nose, and had his head thrown back in a laugh.

"That's from the eighth-grade musical, *You're a Good Man, Charlie Brown*. Ryan was Snoopy."

"Ryan did musicals?" Marissa asked.

"He quit when we got to high school," Theresa told her, checking out the picture over Marissa's shoulder. "I was Peppermint Patty," she added, smiling wistfully at the memory.

Marissa glanced at the other girl. "You sound like you really miss him."

"He just left, you know? One day he was there and the next? His house was empty, and he was gone."

"I don't think he planned any of it," Marissa said softly, but Theresa just shrugged.

"Guess they don't have phones up in Newport Beach," she said, and went back to peeling potatoes.

When Ryan and Arturo came back into the

kitchen a few minutes later, Marissa had picked up a dish towel and was drying glasses, even though Theresa hadn't said another word to her.

"So, I'll be back in half an hour," Ryan said to her, and Marissa set the glass down with a bang.

"You're leaving me here?" she asked. Theresa looked up sharply, and Marissa felt a tiny bit guilty about the way that sounded, but still. "I'm going with you."

"Marissa, hey, you should just go home. Take the car, I'll find a way home."

They walked out to the driveway, Theresa trailing a little behind. Marissa moved to get into Kirsten's car, then saw that Ryan was hesitating, looking at Theresa. Marissa felt a flash of jealousy — she wanted to grab Ryan's arm and pull him away from Theresa, kiss him so hard he would forget Theresa even existed, shove him into the back of the car and lock the doors and drive him so far away from Chino that he could never come back.

But she couldn't do any of those things, so she simply unlocked Kirsten's car and slid into the driver's seat, hoping against hope that the uneasy feeling bubbling up in the pit of her stomach was from hunger and not a premonition of losing Ryan to his old life.

Ryan, meanwhile, was trying to think up something to say to Theresa that would let her know how sorry he was for the way he handled things, without giving her any false hope that he would someday come back to Chino. Because even being here for the half hour it had taken them to get Trey's car up and running had left Ryan panicky and sweating. Nothing about Chino still felt like home, and as much as he had once cared for Theresa, the memories she brought back were things he'd prefer to forget.

But she had such a wounded, hopeful look in her eyes that he couldn't bear to let her down any further. "I'll see you around sometime," he mumbled, his hand on the door handle of Trey's old Camaro.

Theresa forced a smile, willing her tears not to fall until Ryan was out of her life again. "Uh-huh. Good luck."

"You, too," Ryan said, "and, you know, sorry."

A tear escaped, so Theresa turned and ran into the house, unable to answer.

Ryan sighed and got into the car, then looked over to see Marissa, who was staring down at her steering wheel, an unwilling witness to what had just happened. She glanced up and gave him a little wave. And just that was enough to make Ryan feel a little bit better.

He pulled up next to her, rolled down his window. "Okay, I'll call you when I get back?"

Marissa nodded, then threw her car into drive, heading away from Chino.

* * *

Gattas apparently didn't believe in taking holidays off, because when Ryan pulled into the garage with Trey's car, a full crew of thuggy-looking workers was tearing apart a couple of cars up on lifts.

"You Ryan?" Gattas, wiry and mean, with tattoos running up both arms like multicolored sleeves, walked over to Trey's car and popped the hood.

Ryan got out of the car. He tossed the keys to Gattas and started toward the street, but Gattas called after him.

"Hard to believe your dumb-ass brother managed to nick a ride as nice as this," Gattas drawled.

Ryan turned and nodded, still backing toward the street. "We good? You take the car and Trey's off the hook?"

"Oh, is that the deal?" A sneer spread across Gattas's face. "I been waiting for this for six months. There's something called interest."

"I don't have anything," Ryan said, glancing nervously at Gattas's thugs, who were watching the conversation with something like amusement.

"Well, late payments need to be collected," Gattas said and, with no warning, hauled off and punched Ryan in the face.

Ryan let out a yelp, clutching at his bloodied nose with one hand, while desperately searching the room for an escape route. Suddenly he wished that he had let Marissa follow up. Gattas's crew was pressing in, blocking the garage exit to the street. Gattas grabbed a crowbar and moved steadily toward Ryan, the weapon banging against his thigh. But before he could raise it to swing again, there was a squealing of tires as Marissa plowed her car into the garage.

The thugs jumped out of the way to keep from getting hit, and in the split second that Gattas was caught off guard, Ryan clocked him as hard as he could, then leaped for the open passenger door. He dove inside Kirsten's car, and before the door was even shut behind him, Marissa was already peeling out, heading away from Chino as fast as she could go.

"Are you okay?" she asked.

"What are you —?"

"I followed you," Marissa replied.

"You followed me?" Ryan thought about it for a minute. "Good idea," he finally responded, sinking deeper into the SUV's upholstery.

A sudden thought popped into Ryan's head: He was in love with Marissa. The realization surprised him. He'd never told any girl he loved her in his entire life. Not Theresa, not even his *mom*. But here he was thinking it. He wasn't ready to say the words out loud, but he hugged them to himself. One day, he'd be ready to tell her.

For now, they needed to get home for Thanksgiving dinner, but first Ryan had one more stop to make.

"The car's delivered. The debt is paid. But I'm never doing anything for you again. Understand?"

Ryan leaned across the table at the Chino Correctional Facility and stared his brother in the eye.

Trey let his gaze move past Ryan to the bench where Marissa was seated, pretending to be interested in a back issue of *Field & Stream*. He smiled wistfully, recognizing what a good thing his little brother had going, and moved his eyes back to Ryan. "I understand," he said.

As they left Chino and headed back toward the O.C., Ryan was silent, gazing through the windshield at the darkening street in front of him. Marissa followed his lead and didn't say a word. But she also didn't let go of his hand the whole way home.

16

Thanksgiving officially kicked off the holiday season, and for the residents of Newport Beach, that meant parties. The only problem was that Julie Cooper was on the planning committee for a majority of the Christmas festivities in Newport Beach, and Marissa was in no mood to deal with her mother. Especially not if she was going to be showing up at events with Caleb Nichol.

On the surface, things were looking up for Marissa. She was so happy in her relationship with Ryan; ever since they'd come back from Chino they'd been inseparable. She picked him up from the Cohens' every morning before school, they sat together in class and ate lunch in the quad with Seth every day, and they spent most of their evenings together, too.

When she wasn't hanging out with Ryan, Marissa had started to develop a comfortable routine at her dad's new apartment. Jimmy was making a conscious effort to keep food in the fridge, and Marissa made a stab at decorating it to make it feel more homey. A couple of throw pillows and candles were a far cry form the palatial estate they had lived in with Julie, but at least it gave the apartment a feeling of permanence, like Marissa was there to stay.

But as good as things seemed, Marissa just couldn't shake the sense of unease that had started when she met Theresa. Hell, that had started back in Tijuana. Part of it stemmed from her absolute dread of having to face her mother again. Even saying hello on the phone when Julie called to talk to Jimmy about money or the house gave Marissa a stomachache. But now with three weeks of parties coming up? She'd probably end up with an ulcer.

At night, when she couldn't sleep, which lately seemed like every night, she'd lie in bed listening for the sound of her father going into his room, shutting the door, lying down on the bed. She'd wait until she was sure he'd fallen asleep, passing the time by counting the tiles on the ceiling, then slip into the living room. She'd kneel down in front of Jimmy's liquor cabinet and decide which bottle it was safest to take a few drinks from that night.

She was surprised that Jimmy hadn't noticed the steadily declining levels of alcohol in all of the bottles, but Marissa supposed that since he had no reason to suspect her, it didn't even occur to him to check. And she was careful, never taking more than a quarter inch from any one bottle at a time. Some of the liquor was really gross — she couldn't imagine why anyone in their right mind would ever actually choose to drink Southern Comfort, but basically *anything* mixed with orange juice went down easy. Besides, she couldn't just drink his vodka — that he would notice.

If she'd thought about it, Marissa might have been worried about how much she was drinking, and how much fiercer her desire for a drink was growing each night. And sometimes she thought back to the therapist she had talked to when she was in the hospital who seemed so concerned when Marissa told her about sneaking drinks. The whole thing really was sort of unsettling if she thought about it. So Marissa simply chose not to think about it, just poured another drink, and hoped that maybe that would be enough to let her fall asleep.

Seth loved the holidays, and this year he had two reasons to really look forward to them: Summer and Anna. It had all started at Thanksgiving when both girls had decided to come over — Summer just inviting herself. Seth still shivered a little when he thought about how it might all have turned out.

He had been looking forward to Thanksgiving dinner — turkey and all the trimmings — with his family and Anna. He'd been in training for days, eating as much as he could to stretch his stomach so he could make the most of all the food. It was going to be great. Then Ryan got the phone call from his brother and had to leave. He promised to be back in time for dinner so dinner would be late, but Seth figured he wouldn't starve. Meanwhile,

Anna was getting to know his parents and Seth couldn't get over how smart she was. It really was great.

Then the doorbell rang and Seth found Summer standing outside.

"What are you doing here?" Seth asked, stunned.

"Trying to have Thanksgiving. I was supposed to meet Marissa at her house," Summer replied, looking and sounding annoyed. "And while I'm here, I thought maybe we could talk. About what didn't happen on the yacht . . . so, are you going to invite me in?"

"Umm, let's talk in the pool house," Seth said quickly. "Let's go round this way — we put gardenias in the front lawn. I think you'll be impressed."

Summer had stared at Seth like he was nuts, but followed in his wake. Seth couldn't explain it but he didn't want Summer in the house while Anna was there. It just felt wrong. He'd invited Anna to dinner and he didn't want to spoil that. But at the same time, he couldn't abandon Summer. He needed a plan.

With Summer safely stashed in the pool house, Seth had gone back inside the house, where he found Anna looking for him.

"Where you been?" she asked.

"Ryan asked me to feed his Sea Monkeys while he was away," Seth improvised.

"Ryan has Sea Monkeys? Those things are cool," Anna said, starting to head toward the back door. "Maybe we could check them out . . . and have a little privacy . . ."

"They're dead!" Seth said quickly. "It was a terrible tragedy. Why don't I show you my room?"

Upstairs, Anna had inspected his room, met Captain Oats, and then begun to kiss him. It was nice. Very nice. But a little voice at the back of Seth's mind kept saying that this was going to get complicated. Very complicated.

After a quick call to Ryan for advice, which he didn't have, Seth ran back out to the pool house. Summer practically jumped him. Before Seth knew what was happening, he was lying on Ryan's bed, making out with Summer. *Summer!* He couldn't believe it.

Suddenly, Summer pushed him off the bed. "We shouldn't be doing this," she said, "it shouldn't be happening. I must be lightheaded. I need something to eat. Let's go inside —"

"No!" Seth cried from the floor. "I mean, you're the guest. I'm the host. I should go. I'll get us something to eat."

And with that he ran into the house and up to his room where Anna was playing Jenga with Captain Oats. She was winning against the plastic horse, but getting bored with the game. Before Seth knew it, he and Anna were lying on his bed kissing. But before he could get too carried away, he remembered Summer back in the pool house. Making an excuse about checking on the potatoes, he ran downstairs — straight into his dad. Waiting for him. Busted. Then Summer and Anna entered the room, both having gotten tired of waiting for Seth. Busted big time. They looked at each other. Hurt. They looked at Seth. Hurt and maybe a little angry. Then they both turned and walked away.

"You can't lead these girls on," Sandy said once he'd heard the whole story. "You have to tell them the truth."

The problem was that Seth didn't know what the truth was. He liked them both . . . a lot. Anna was funny and smart and sweet and cute. And Summer was . . . Summer. He needed a plan. A really good plan.

With all the Christmas parties coming up, Seth's only worry was how he would behave when he was in a room with both of them. He didn't want Summer to see him together with Anna, because that might make her stop liking him. But at the same time, he didn't want to hurt Anna by trying to get closer to Summer. And if Summer never fully came around, he wanted Anna there as a backup. Although, when he thought about it, that sounded mean. And Seth never ever wanted to be mean, especially not to Anna.

So he'd need a plan, but who'd have ever thought he'd need a plan for this kind of situation. Seth Cohen and two girls! Life was good.

Ryan was feeling ambivalent about the approaching holidays. Holidays in Chino had always had more than their fair share of family drama, usually ending up with his mom passed out, no food on the table, and Trey or his mom's latest boyfriend threatening to kick Ryan's ass. Now he was about to experience the Newport holiday season, and he had a feeling that it wouldn't be anything like the Chino one. On top of that, he had no money to buy presents, but he'd decided not to worry about that one . . . yet.

Apart from a certain pre-holiday dread, however, things were going pretty well. Things were good with Marissa, good with the Cohens, and all his hard work studying at Thanksgiving had really paid off — he came back to school fully caught up with his homework, got A's on a couple of pop quizzes in trig and biology, and even managed to pull off a B on his English paper.

Sandy was so proud of him that he took him to a Lakers game, just the two of them, and afterward they sat in a diner, eating burgers and talking about basketball. It was the sort of evening Ryan had only dreamed about having with his own father, and it made him feel closer to Sandy than ever before.

Nothing could mar his happiness, not even the announcement in history class that for their next project, the teacher would be assigning them to two-person teams to report on pivotal moments in European history. Marissa, who was sitting next to Ryan, slipped him a note: "Should we do the Crusades?" but the teacher had a different idea.

"Jennifer and Laura: the Protestant Reformation. Marissa and Paige: the French Revolution . . ." Marissa shot a disappointed glance at Ryan, who smiled and shrugged. Would have been nice to be partners, but he'd work with whomever he was assigned. "Ryan and Luke: the Spanish Inquisition."

Luke? Shit. He should have known that things were too good to last.

17

Luke's house was built on the edge a cliff overlooking the ocean, and Ryan stood on the front stoop, deliberating whether throwing himself over the edge onto the rocks below would be a less painful evening than actually ringing the doorbell.

"Let's get this over with," Ryan muttered to himself, and knocked. A moment later, the door was opened by a tall, athletic man who looked like Luke, only a quarter century older.

"You must be Luke's friend," the man said, and smiled. "I'm Luke's dad. You can call me Carson."

"Ryan," Ryan said, shaking Carson's hand. He smiled back, as much out of amusement at being called Luke's "friend" as anything else. "We're doing a history project together."

"On what?"

"The Spanish Inquisition."

"Not one of Western civilization's proudest moments," Carson said with a grin.

Ryan started to answer, but then Luke appeared, hostility clear on his face. "Are we gonna do this?" he asked Ryan, who nodded. "Later, Dad."

"Good luck," Carson said, giving Ryan a wink. He started to leave, then turned back. "Hey, S.C.–Notre Dame game this Sunday. Figured we'd drive up around noon, tailgate."

"Cool," Luke answered.

"I don't know if you're a Trojan man, Ryan, but it's gonna be a good game."

"Thanks —" Ryan started, but Luke cut him off.

"He's got plans Sunday, right?"

"Yeah," Ryan said, and sighed. The evening couldn't end soon enough. Luke's dad clattered out the door on his way back to work, and Luke looked at Ryan.

"We can work in my room. I found a bunch of sites online that we can use."

He turned and jogged up the stairs and Ryan followed. He was sure what he was expecting Luke's room to look like — maybe weight machines, sports trophies, surfing gear. There was some of that, but there were also a couple of acoustic guitars and tons of sheet music. Dave Matthews, John Mayer, James Taylor. It was a completely unexpected side of Luke. But when Ryan picked up the music to "You've Got a Friend," Luke snatched it out of his hands.

"Let's just get to work, okay?"

"Fine," Ryan said. He pulled a bunch of books he'd gotten from the library out of his backpack and settled down on the bed. "Maybe we should start with the palace of the Grand Inquisitor in Toledo and go from there. . . ."

Luke nodded, typing the keywords into his computer, and for the next two hours, they buckled down.

By the time they had nailed down the official church policy on the inquisitor's methods, both boys were ready for a break. They went down to Luke's kitchen, where he poured them each a glass of iced tea, then rummaged around in a cabinet until he unearthed a bag of Oreos.

"My mom has to keep these hidden, or my little brothers will devour them," he told Ryan, stuffing a handful of the cookies into his mouth.

Ryan twisted an Oreo in half, licking off the filling like a little kid. He couldn't believe how cool Luke was being. It made sense, when he thought about it. Marissa wouldn't have gone out with Luke if he were a total jerk. Ryan had just never seen his nice side before. Hell, if they had to keep working together, he and Luke might even become friends.

"I was thinking we could do a slide show on my Powerbook," Luke was saying. "My dad has a film scanner down at his office, with Power Point and a color Laserjet. We could head over there and do some more work."

"Sounds good," Ryan said.

The boys climbed into Luke's Lexus SUV. "This is, like, the nicest car I've ever been in," Ryan said. Luke's teeth flashed as he grinned.

"My dad owns a dealership. Otherwise there's no way . . ."

They got to Carson's showroom, and Luke unlocked the door. "Dad? You here? Hello?" Luke called. There was no answer, so Luke shrugged. "I guess he's gone."

Ryan wasn't paying attention, though. He was too busy checking out all the gorgeous new cars that were parked on the showroom floor.

"Man, do you get to drive all these?"

"Not that one!" Luke said, pointing at the little roadster Ryan was admiring. "That's an eighty-thousand-dollar car."

"Damn." Ryan bent down for a closer look, then spotted Carson through the doorway to the sales office, talking to another man.

"Hey, there's your dad."

Luke looked to where he was pointing. "Oh, that's Gus, his business partner. We should go say hi."

The boys started across the floor, but then stopped abruptly as Carson took Gus's hand and pulled him into a passionate embrace. Luke watched, horrified, as his dad kissed another man, then turned and ran, grabbing Ryan's shirt and pulling him out to the parking lot.

"If you tell anyone," Luke threatened, his voice coming in ragged gasps.

"I won't," Ryan promised, but Luke turned away.

"You better not."

18

Ryan spent a restless night, and when Marissa swung by the pool house to pick him up for school, he was still gathering his books together.

"How did it go last night? You didn't call me," she said, wrapping her arms around his neck and giving him a kiss.

"Yeah, we were working pretty late, so . . ." Ryan trailed off. He pulled away from her embrace and zipped up his backpack. Marissa looked at him oddly, sensing something was up.

"What happened?"

"Nothing."

"Ryan." Marissa put her hands on her hips. "I can tell that something happened. Did you guys talk about me?"

"No." Ryan couldn't meet her eyes.

"What did you say about me?"

"Nothing, okay? God."

He and Marissa stared at each other for a minute, then she turned away. "Fine." She started toward the door, clearly annoyed, and Ryan touched her shoulder.

"Wait. Something happened last night, but it's not about you, and I promised Luke I wouldn't say anything."

"What is it?" Marissa asked, obviously dying of curiosity.

Ryan shook his head.

"You can tell me," she said. "I won't say anything."

"Okay," Ryan said, relieved to be able to share this burden, "but you can't tell anyone. Not even Summer. *Especially* not Summer."

"I won't. I swear."

"Luke's dad kissed another guy."

Marissa blinked. She must have heard that wrong. "What? What are you talking about?"

"Luke's dad was making out with another guy. We saw them."

"Oh my god —"

"But you can't tell anyone."

"I — won't. . . ." Marissa said, and Ryan smiled.

"Great." He glanced at his watch, then picked up his backpack. "C'mon. We're going to be late."

He started toward the door, leaving Marissa behind him, still reeling from the news.

When they got to school, the first thing they saw was Luke standing by his locker, talking to a couple of his friends from the rugby team.

"I'm gonna go talk to him," Ryan murmured to

Marissa, and she nodded, squeezing his hand and then heading off toward her own locker.

Ryan wasn't sure what he was going to say to Luke, but he wanted to check in with him, make sure he was doing okay and reassure him that his secret was safe. But as he approached, Luke turned to face him, a sneer on his face.

"What do *you* want?" he asked, hatred in his voice.

"Uh, I just wanted to talk about —"

"We have nothing to talk about," Luke stopped him.

Jerk. "— finishing our project," Ryan finished in a level voice.

But Luke just turned back to his locker, abruptly dismissing Ryan. "I'll do it myself. Now stay the hell away from me."

Luke's friends laughed as Ryan slunk away. Guess he should have expected that Luke wouldn't want to be reminded that someone else knew his dad's secret. It was too bad, though. Last night it had seemed like they might actually get along.

The rest of the day passed without incident, and Ryan decided the best course of action was to pretend that nothing had happened, and it would all blow over. He was sure Luke was going to have a rough time of it, but hey, he'd made an effort, and what happened between Luke and his dad really wasn't his problem.

He and Marissa didn't discuss it again that day,

and the next morning when they arrived at school, Ryan was fully expecting everything to be back to normal. He couldn't have been more wrong.

"Did you guys hear about Luke's dad?" Summer asked, rushing across the student parking lot to meet them. "Omigod, Coop, I couldn't believe it."

Marissa looked at Ryan, wanting to commiserate over the fact that the secret was out, but instead she was shocked to see fury spreading over his face.

"Who did you tell?" he demanded.

Marissa shook her head in denial. "Nobody."

"I asked you not to say anything —"

"I didn't!" Marissa insisted. She couldn't believe what she was hearing. How could Ryan think she would blab after he'd asked her not to? She wouldn't do that to him. God, she especially wouldn't do that to Luke. As much as she hated him for cheating on her, she would never gossip about something that had such potential to hurt him.

"I never should have told you in the first place," Ryan continued. "God, I can't believe I trusted you."

Marissa took a step back, as startled as if he'd physically struck her. How did this happen? Who could have spilled the secret? She tried to think of an answer for Ryan, but she was as angry and upset as he was.

Before she could think up the right words to say, they were interrupted by Luke, who came barreling across the parking lot, his eyes red, his face set in a mask of rage.

"Who did you tell?!!" He grabbed Ryan's shirt, pulling him close as though he were going to beat a confession out of him.

In the parking lot around them, kids were whispering and giggling, sending pointedly malicious glances at Luke.

But Ryan stood limply, not putting up any sort of defenses for the first time in his life. Because he *had* told someone. It was his fault that Luke's secret was out. "I'm sorry," he said quietly.

Luke's face screwed up with the effort of not bursting into tears. He slammed Ryan backward, throwing him into the side of Marissa's car. "You're dead," he said, then turned and ran back to his own car, the beautiful SUV throwing up gravel as Luke squealed away.

Ryan, Marissa, and Summer all stood helplessly, watching him leave.

19

Marissa didn't get a lot of work done in school that day. She felt terrible for Luke, and she was so angry at Ryan that she didn't know what to do. She hadn't said a word to anyone, and it was completely unfair of him not to trust her. All she had done since she met him was look for ways to build his trust, and now everything was being ruined, and it wasn't even her fault. She and her dad were supposed to have dinner at the Cohens' that night, but Marissa didn't know if she wanted to see him. She couldn't handle sitting across from his accusatory stare all night. Especially at a party with her parents, where she couldn't even sneak a drink to take off the edge.

She figured she'd probably just spend the evening lying on her bed, feeling sorry for herself, but when Jimmy got home, he was in such a cheerful mood that she didn't have the heart to complain.

"Ready, sweetheart?" he asked her, looking in the mirror and fiddling with the ridiculous Santa

Claus tie that Marissa had given him for Christmas when she was eight. He wore it every year over Julie's protests, freely admitting that it was the tackiest thing around.

"I guess," Marissa answered, reaching up to help him get the knot straight.

"You don't seem very jolly," he said, taking in his daughter's long face. "Trouble in paradise?"

"Ryan and I are fighting," she said.

"You want to talk about it?" Jimmy asked, studying his reflection. He smoothed his hair back and gave his tie a final tug.

"No," Marissa answered gloomily. "He's just being a jerk."

"That's men for you," Jimmy said, shaking his head sympathetically, and Marissa couldn't help but smile.

"Dad, you're such a goofball."

"I know," he said, and gave her a quick kiss on top of her head. "Now let's go make merry."

Marissa rolled her eyes but let her dad lead her out the door and to the Cohens'.

She was nervous about what she'd say to Ryan when he opened the door, but she needn't have been. Ryan wasn't even home.

"I think he's gone crazy," Seth told her in a low voice, after Jimmy had gone into the kitchen with Sandy and Kirsten and the kids were alone. "He told me he was going over to Luke's."

"Oh god," Marissa said, the pain in her stomach starting to spread. She really wished she had a drink.

Ryan, meanwhile, had arrived at Luke's house with no plan other than to apologize again for ruining Luke's life, and was surprised when, instead of punching him, Luke asked if he maybe wanted to drive down to the baseball field and hang out.

"My dad told my mom the truth," he said by way of explanation. "She told some friends in her yoga class, and that's how it got all over town. So . . . I owe you an apology."

"No, man, it's fine," Ryan said. He felt as uncomfortable as he could ever remember being, but there was no way he was leaving. Ryan had had enough trouble in his life to know how much it could help just having someone to listen.

They pulled up to the field and got out. Luke grabbed a six-pack of beer from the trunk and smiled ruefully at Ryan. "My dad's. Guess he won't yell at me for drinking it."

The two boys walked down to the dugout and sat down on the players' bench.

"It's like everything in my life has been a lie. How am I ever going to believe another word anyone says to me? I feel completely abandoned," Luke said, and polished off a bottle.

Ryan handed him another, and opened a second for himself, too. "I know how you feel," he said quietly, and Luke stopped, momentarily taken out of his own grief by what Ryan had said.

"Yeah, I guess you do."

"Here's to messed-up families," Ryan said with a small smile, and they clinked bottles.

Luke drained his beer in three gulps and was reaching for a third when movement on the baseball field caught his eye.

"Look," he said in a low voice to Ryan, setting down his bottle and getting to his feet.

Six guys in Del Vista letter jackets were walking across the field toward them. Del Vista was the local public school and a notorious Harbor rival.

"Isn't this romantic?" one of the Del Vista guys said. He had long floppy hair and the faintest wispy beginnings of a beard.

"Leave us alone, guys," Ryan said. There were too many of them to fight, so he said a futile prayer that the guys would just go away.

"Aw, you want to be alone with your boyfriend?" the guy asked, and his friends all laughed.

Ryan could feel Luke tensing beside him, so he thought he'd give diplomacy one more shot.

"Seriously, guys, why don't you get out of here?" he said, and wispy beard took a step closer.

"What are you going to do, call your daddy for help?" he asked in a lisping baby voice.

Luke lifted his fist to slug the guy, but before he could get his arm back, Ryan had already flattened the guy, knocking him to the ground with one clean punch, and was turning toward wispy's friend.

"Asshole —" the guy started, and Luke punched him as hard as he could, focusing all his own pain into the satisfying crack of the Del Vista guy's nose shattering. Ryan and Luke shared a quick look — they were actually on the same side in a fight! It was unprecedented. They gave each other a quick smile, which vanished as the remaining four Del Vista players moved in.

Dinner was well under way by the time a bleeding Ryan and Luke staggered up the driveway. Sandy and Kirsten had not been thrilled when Ryan didn't show up on time, but they'd heard about Luke's dad, so they were prepared to cut him some slack.

The adults were all talking and laughing, but Marissa was staring down at her plate, glumly pushing a piece of broccoli back and forth, and Seth was trying to figure out a way to find out just how much of their illicit kiss Summer had told Marissa about. He had made a couple of false starts, but every way he could think of to approach the question seemed to lead to Marissa telling Summer and Summer getting mad at him. If she hadn't told Marissa about the kiss, he was pretty sure she wouldn't want Seth to tell her. Especially because it was less than a week before the Newport Group holiday party, and he was going with both Anna *and* Summer, so he didn't want anyone mad at him.

He had just about worked up his courage to ask her flat out what Summer thought about him, when the door opened and Ryan and Luke stumbled in.

"Oh my god," Kirsten cried, leaping to her feet.

The adults rushed over to them, helping Luke, who had been propped up on Ryan's shoulder, to the couch.

"I didn't do it this time," Ryan said, and Sandy put a reassuring hand on his shoulder.

"Here, sit down. Are you okay?"

"Some Del Vista morons jumped us," Ryan said, "but we're okay."

"You're bleeding pretty bad," Kirsten told Luke, gently pushing his hair back off his forehead to examine the cut above his eye. "Let's go into the bathroom and get you cleaned up."

Sandy and Kirsten led him into the bathroom, and Jimmy picked up the phone. "I'm going to call your parents and let them know where you are," he said.

Luke hesitated. "I'd really rather not see them right now, if that's okay," he said.

"We'll just tell them you're okay," Jimmy promised, and went off into the living room to make the call, leaving Ryan with Marissa and Seth.

"Okay, what really happened?" Seth asked, but Ryan didn't answer. He and Marissa were staring at each other.

Seth looked back and forth at the two of them and sighed. "I'm going to go call Anna," he said, and escaped to his room, leaving the other two alone together.

Once Seth was gone, Marissa moved to Ryan, gently touching his bruised face with her fingertips. "Are you sure you're okay?" she whispered.

"I'm sorry," Ryan said. "I never should have doubted you."

"You can trust me, you know," Marissa said, still stroking his cheek.

"I do," Ryan answered. He captured her hand with his own, brought it to his mouth, kissed her fingers. "Can you forgive me?"

Marissa shrugged, smiling. "Well, you were pretty great with Luke today. You don't even like him."

Now it was Ryan who shrugged. "He's not so bad," he said.

"So you guys are friends now? You're going to hang out, do guy stuff, talk about me?"

"What makes you think we haven't already?" Ryan teased.

"Ryan!" Marissa said, slapping him on the shoulder.

Ryan winced, laughing. "Ouch! That's where the Del Vista guys got me."

"Serves you right," Marissa said. She moved to hit him again, and he tackled her, laughing and kissing, onto the couch.

Jimmy arranged for Luke to spend the night at the Cohens', and the next morning Marissa came and picked the three guys up for school.

They parked Marissa's car and walked down the path to the quad, where their classmates were all gathered, waiting for the morning bell to ring. Luke hesitated, hanging back behind the other kids, so they all stopped, supporting him.

"This is going to be weird," Luke said, and Ryan nodded.

"Yep."

"Everybody's going to be staring at me, talking. . . ." Luke continued anxiously.

"Yep," Marissa said, flashing Ryan a smile.

"Maybe I should blow off today," Luke said. "Go to the beach or something and give everybody a chance to just get it out of their systems."

"It doesn't work like that," Ryan told him. "It's been months and I'm still the kid from Chino who was in juvie."

"I'm still the girl who tried to kill herself in Mexico," Marissa said.

"And I'm still . . . Seth Cohen," Seth added.

Luke looked at them, then back out at the crowd of kids on the wide lawn. "Man, this is gonna suck."

Seth slapped him on the back. "Welcome to my world."

And with that, Ryan, Seth, Luke, and Marissa shared a brief smile before bravely heading into the quad together, ready for whatever the day would hold.

20

"Allow me to introduce you to a little something I like to call . . . Chrismukkah," Seth said, tossing Ryan a candy cane.

"Chrismukkah?" Ryan asked.

"That's right. The new holiday that's sweeping the nation. At least the living room. It's the best of both worlds."

Just then the front door flew open and a huge Christmas tree appeared. From somewhere within the tree, Sandy could be heard calling for help. Ryan rushed over to lend a hand and in a few minutes the tree was standing in the living room.

Seth, meanwhile, was still going on about Chrismukkah. "It's the greatest super-holiday known to man. Drawing on the bet that Christianity and Judaism have to offer." He finished pointing at Kirsten and Sandy.

Ryan was uncomfortable. There were no At-wood family traditions, unless you counted his mom getting drunk and him getting his butt kicked by her boyfriend of the moment. Ryan looked at the Cohens, who were all waiting for him to say something.

"Well, whatever you want me to do . . . I'll do." He smiled and quickly exited the room.

Seth glanced after Ryan then turned to his parents. "Soon, Ryan shall learn the magic of Chrismukkah. I shall convert him. Now let's decorate the tree."

Now Ryan had a new worry, what to get the Cohens for Chrismukkah. He wanted something meaningful, which would let them know exactly how much he appreciated being a part of their family, but at the same time, he was practically broke, and it seemed really sleazy to borrow money from Sandy to buy him his own present. He hoped that with Marissa's help, he could find the perfect gift.

So that Saturday, Ryan and Marissa headed to the galleria to do some Christmas shopping. Their first stop was the Orange County Neiman Marcus. Ryan couldn't believe the sort of crap people wasted their money on. Monogrammed dog food bowls. Purses shaped like big pieces of bubble gum. Six-hundred-dollar water bottle holders. Ryan couldn't imagine ever finding anything Kirsten and Sandy would like in a store like this.

But Marissa was right at home. She trailed her fingers through a bin of silk scarves, held a pair of gigantic emeralds up to her ears and admired herself in the mirror, smoothed some bright red gloss onto her lips. Maybe his earlier feeling that things ere going to be okay had just been a mistake.

Ryan watched her with a smile.

"Finding a lot of stuff you like?" he asked her, and she smiled, putting the lipstick back down and picking up a heavy nautical watch.

"I can't really afford this place anymore," she said wistfully, and checked out the price tag on the timepiece. "Nine hundred dollars."

"Yeah, it's a pretty nice watch," Ryan said, "but I bet we can find something just as good at the ninety-nine-cent store down the block."

"I guess," Marissa said, "but I like it here. Everything's so perfect that you feel like all your problems could be solved if you only had the right lipstick or a new pair of shoes."

They moved toward the exit, taking the elevators two flights down to the parking garage. But as they approached Marissa's car, a security guard hurried toward them.

"Miss? I'm going to have to ask to see your purse," he demanded. Marissa shot a helpless look at Ryan, who stepped forward.

"You've made a mistake," he started, but the guard ignored him.

"If you don't hand over your purse right now, I'll have no choice but to call the police."

With trembling fingers, Marissa handed her purse to the guard, who upended it on the hood of her car. Along with her wallet and sunglasses, out fell the lip gloss she had tried on, one of the pretty silk scarves, and the nine-hundred-dollar watch. Ryan stared in disbelief, as Marissa dropped her head and started to cry.

The security guards wouldn't let Ryan wait with Marissa for Jimmy to come pick her up, so she handed him her car keys and told him she would see him that night. Ryan drove slowly home through the festively decorated streets, turning over the day's proceedings in his mind. Christmas in Chino had never been a very joyful affair. He and Theresa usually exchanged gifts, and that was frequently the only bright spot in an otherwise astonishingly unpleasant day. More years than not, his mom would have drunk away whatever money she'd set aside, and any expectations of a merry Christmas would be quickly dashed by tears and fighting and drunken accusations.

So far life at the Cohen household showed a lot more promise — Seth was a self-appointed jolly elf, hanging stockings and wrapping gifts and wandering into the kitchen repeatedly to make sure there would be enough cookies and eggnog to last through New Year's. But Marissa getting detained today felt like a bad omen — it was the start of trouble, just like on every other Christmas of his life. Maybe his earlier feeling that things were going to be okay had just been a mistake.

Marissa slumped on a bench in the department store security office, dreading her dad showing up. There was a fat mean-looking kid sitting next to her who had also been caught stealing, and his huge meaty leg kept pushing against hers. Marissa scooted to the very edge of the bench, trying to get away from him. A radio played a tinny version of "Deck the Halls," and the bored-looking female officer doing paperwork at her desk while she watched over the detainees sang along with the "fa-la-la's" under her breath.

It seemed like hours before Jimmy got there, so by the time the door opened and he walked in, Marissa felt like she was going to faint from relief. That emotion was short-lived, because right behind him was Julie Cooper.

"I can't believe you called her," Marissa said to her dad, and Julie's nostrils flared with anger.

"You do not get to say one word, young lady," she hissed. "Stealing? Like a common criminal? How could you, Marissa?"

"Let's talk about this calmly," Jimmy said, and Julie turned her anger on him.

"Oh, you would forgive this," she said. "It's pretty obvious where she learned to steal."

"God, stop it!" cried Marissa. "I'm the one to blame for this, not Dad."

"Well, we'll see what your new therapist has to say about this."

"Mom, no! I'm not talking to a therapist. I'm not crazy." When Julie didn't answer, Marissa turned to Jimmy for help. "Dad —"

"Sorry, kiddo, but I'm with your mom on this

one." He knelt down in front of the bench where she was sitting, so their eyes were level. "Look, obviously there's something going on, and maybe if you have someone to talk to, things can get better."

"They'll get better if she leaves me alone," Marissa said, casting a dark glance at her mother, but Julie ignored her.

"We have a party to get ready for, so I suggest —"

"You're still going to make me go to the stupid Newport Group party?" Marissa asked plaintively, and Julie nodded.

"I have spent a lot of time planning this event, and I will not be embarrassed by having my own daughter miss it. Now, you will go tonight and smile and be polite to all my friends, and tomorrow morning I will personally drive you to Dr. Milano's office."

"Whatever," Marissa said in a petulant voice.

Julie softened, putting a hand on her daughter's arm. "Honey. I love you. I am just trying to help you —"

"We should get going," Marissa snapped. "After all, you don't want to keep Caleb waiting."

Without another glance at her mother, Marissa swept out of the room. Jimmy and Julie exchanged a glance, but had no choice but to follow.

21

The Newport Group offices that night looked as lovely as anyone had ever seen. Tiny white lights glinted in all the trees, while the windows were wrapped in huge swaths of red and green velvet.

Seth walked in with his parents and headed right for the dessert table. He piled a little china plate with as many cookies as would fit, then wandered off to find Ryan, who had come separately, driving Marissa's car.

But instead of Ryan, he bumped into Anna, who was all dolled up in a slinky red dress. "Mistletoe," she said brightly, holding a sprig of green up over their heads. Seth grinned and leaned forward to kiss her.

"You are looking very fetching tonight," he told her.

"Thank you."

"So — would you mind fetching me some more cookies?"

Anna laughed and took his empty plate from him. "Only if you fetch us some punch."

"It's a plan," Seth said, and headed toward the bar.

But before he got there, Summer came up to him, a sly smile on her face.

"Cohen," she said seriously. "I've decided to start my resolutions a week early. And my first one? Is you."

Seth blinked, his mouth suddenly very dry. "So — you're saying — what exactly are you saying?"

"Mistletoe!" Summer said and, pulling the exact same trick Anna had, held a sprig over their heads. She rose up on tiptoe to kiss him, and Seth kissed her back, hyperconscious of the fact that Anna was on her way back to meet him.

"Um, I actually think that's holly," he said somewhat lamely, pointing at the leaves in Summer's hand when she had finished kissing him.

But instead of getting annoyed at his obtuseness the way she usually would, Summer cocked an eyebrow at him. "Well then, I guess I'd better go find some of the real stuff. Because I plan to keep you under it all night."

She traced a seductive finger down the front of his shirt, then turned and walked off, confident that his eyes were following her.

Seth gulped. He really wanted to be friends with both Anna and Summer, but it was getting obvious that they had other ideas. He really needed to find Ryan and get his advice, but instead he found Anna, who pulled him into an empty room.

"Can we talk for a minute?" Seth asked, but she was already in his arms, pressing against him as she kissed him hungrily.

Seth lost some of his resolve. Maybe he could make this work with two girls . . . who was he kidding? No, it had to be friends.

"Anna," he said softly, but she was looking up at him with such a sweet smile that he lost the words.

"I got you a present," she said, reaching into her purse. She pulled out a hand-drawn comic book and gave it to him.

"The Amazing Adventures of Seth Cohen and Captain Oats the Wonder Horse," he read out loud, grinning delightedly at the picture of himself with his trusty sidekick. "You made me a comic? About me?"

"Do you like it?" Anna asked.

"Like it? I love it! This is the best present I ever got. Seriously. I can't believe you made this. Thank you." He swept her up in an embrace.

Anna giggled, tipping her face up to meet his. "Careful not to crush it," she said, nodding at the comic book.

"No way. I'm going to treasure this forever." Seth carefully placed the comic in the inside pocket of his suit jacket. He gave her one more kiss and then, taking her hand, led her back out to the party.

When they got out to the main floor, they saw Anna's father gesturing to her to come meet the people he was talking to.

"Want to come say hi to my dad?" she asked Seth, but he shook his head.

"Later, okay? I still need to find Ryan."

"No probs," Anna said, wiggling her fingers at him as she walked away.

Seth looked around the room — where could Ryan be? He'd come back from shopping with Marissa and gone straight to the pool house without speaking to anyone. Seth had followed him, and Ryan told him everything that had happened that day. He had seemed so depressed about Marissa and the whole holiday season in general that Seth wanted to make sure he was doing all right.

He looked all around, but the only person he managed to find was Summer.

"Hey, Summer," he said, glancing around for Anna. Moments ago he was sure that Anna was the right girl for him, but just being near Summer made his skin prickle.

"Cohen, follow me," Summer ordered, turning and walking toward an unused lounge.

Seth followed, his legs seeming to have a mind of their own. They went into the lounge and Summer shut the door, staring at him expectantly.

"Summer, what are we doing?" Seth started to say, but Summer held up a finger to silence him.

"I hear you like comic books, Cohen," she said, and Seth nodded.

"This is true."

"Merry Christmas," Summer said, and undid

the buttons on her dress. She let it drop to the floor and stood in front of him.

Even in his wildest fantasies, Seth had never imagined the sight that he now beheld: Summer was wearing a Wonder Woman costume, complete with golden lasso.

"Good l-lord," Seth stammered. "I think I'm going to pass out."

Summer tossed the lasso so it fell over Seth's shoulders. "You're not going anywhere." She tugged on the cord, Seth stumbling toward her, and put her arms around him. There was a sudden crackle of paper. Summer leaned back, reaching into Seth's pocket, and pulled out Anna's comic book. "What's this?" she asked him.

"Um, Anna made it. For Christmas."

Summer flipped through the pages, dismay slowly spreading across her face. "She *made* it?"

"Yeah."

"It's amazing," she said quietly. She glanced down at her costume, suddenly self-conscious. Making matters worse, the door to the lounge opened, and Anna stepped into the room.

"Seth? Are you in here?" she called, then stopped short when she saw Seth and Summer.

"Anna! Hey — Summer was just giving me my present," Seth said awkwardly, wriggling out of the lasso.

Anna ignored him, unable to take her eyes off the other girl. "You're Wonder Woman," she said, then her eyes dropped to the comic book that Summer was still clutching. "Is that my comic?"

Summer nodded, handing the book back to Seth.

Anna shook her head in disbelief. "God, I made you a comic. What am I, eight?"

"No, Anna, wait —" Seth said, but she was already moving toward the door.

"You should stay," Summer said to her, struggling back into her dress. "I'll go. I'm sorry."

"It's not your fault," Anna said, then stopped. She and Summer exchanged a look.

"You're right," Summer said. "It's not. And it's not your fault, either."

The girls turned on Seth, having reached a silent agreement. Seth was looking back and forth between the two of them, unsure what was happening but instinctively knowing that it wasn't good.

"Ladies, please," Seth started, but Summer cut him off.

"Listen. I like you," Summer said, then glanced at Anna, "but so does she. And if we don't end this?"

"Someone's going to get hurt," Anna finished.

"You've got to choose between us, Cohen," Summer said, and without another word, the two girls walked out of the room.

Seth watched them go, clueless as to what to do next. He couldn't choose between them, and he didnt want to choose. Why couldn't they be friends?

22

The only thing that got Marissa through the beginning of the evening was the bottle of vodka she
had nicked from her dad's supply. It was a big risk,
but she was past caring. If they were going to make
her go to therapy anyway, she might as well stop
trying to seem normal and just do whatever she
wanted.

She sat in the backseat of Jimmy's car on the
way to the party, refusing to speak to her father.
When they got there, she brushed right past her
mother and headed straight to an upstairs balcony,
where she could watch for Ryan to come in without
running the risk of anyone seeing her.

She was still there, working her way through the
better part of the bottle, when Ryan finally arrived.
She flew down the stairs to greet him, tossing her
arms around his neck and giving him a sloppy kiss.

"There you are! Did you miss me?" she asked,
and Ryan laughed uncertainly, peeling her off him.

"You okay?"

"Mmmm, now that you're here I am," she

128

growled sexily, and tugged at his shirt, untucking it from his pants.

Ryan pulled away for real now, hastily tucking his shirt back in. "Had a few cocktails?" he asked quietly.

Marissa pulled the half-empty bottle of scotch out of her purse and waved it at him, laughing and stumbling against him. "Wanna catch up?" she slurred.

"No," Ryan said, and grabbed her wrist, starting to pull her toward the door. "What are you doing?"

"I'm just having fun," Marissa said.

"Right. The first night I met you, you were having fun passed out in your driveway. A couple of weeks later, it was an alley in Mexico. It's like my mom all over again."

"Shut up," Marissa said, yanking her wrist out of his grasp, but he grabbed it again before she could move away.

"We're getting out of here," he said.

"I am. Enjoy the party." Marissa took a few uneven steps away from him.

"You can't drive," he said, but she wrenched herself away from him and ran out the door. Sighing, Ryan followed her.

Marissa climbed into the front seat of her car and, after a few tries, managed to put the key into the ignition. Ryan ran up to the door, but she slammed down the lock before he could open it. Glaring through the window at him, she threw the car into reverse and backed right into a guardrail, cracking her taillight.

She jerked the car forward, then braked, putting her head down on the steering wheel. Sobs racked her thin shoulders. Ryan knocked lightly on the window, and she popped the lock without looking up.

"Slide over," he said quietly. Then he got into the driver's seat and pulled out of the parking lot.

Marissa stared out the window of the car at the passing mansions of Newport Beach. She snuck a peek at Ryan to make sure he wasn't watching her, then snuck the bottle of scotch out of her purse. She unscrewed the cap and took a gulp, then lowered the bottle to find Ryan looking at her with something like disgust on his face.

"What?" Marissa said, all her defenses up. "You're driving, not me."

"Yeah, because you're drunk."

"I'm not," Marissa insisted.

Ryan blew out his breath. "Put it away," he said.

Marissa started to, but she dropped the cap. It rolled underneath her seat. "Oops."

Ryan turned his attention from her to the rearview mirror and blanched. "Shit." Behind them, a police car turned on its siren, and the colored lights flashed red and blue across their dashboard. "I'm still on probation," he hissed, scowling at Marissa as he pulled over to the side of the road.

Marissa tucked the open bottle between her feet and arranged her dress to drape across it.

The cop came up to the driver's side window, and Ryan handed him his license and the registration.

"You've got a broken taillight," the officer said. "You know that?"

"It just happened, sir. We're going to get it fixed," Ryan answered.

The cop shined his lights inside the car, playing over the kids' faces, and panning across the floor, just missing Marissa's scotch bottle. "You kids been drinking?"

"No sir," Ryan said, and Marissa shook her head.

"Well," the cop said. "Get that light fixed. Happy holidays."

He walked back to his car. But even after he'd pulled away, Ryan didn't start driving. He sat for a minute, his hands squeezing the steering wheel, then got out of the car. He walked over to Marissa's side and opened the door. Then he grabbed the bottle and hurled it away from them. It smashed on the sidewalk. Ryan slammed the door shut, then opened it again. Slammed it again and again. *SLAM! SLAM! SLAM!*

"Stop it!" Marissa said, flinching away from him, the tears starting to course down her face again. "You're scaring me."

"Good!" Ryan shouted. "Because you're scaring me."

131

He slammed the door a final time, then got back in the driver's seat. "If there's drinking, crying, and cops, well then, I guess it must be Christmas." He looked Marissa in the eyes, his expression grave. "I left this behind. I'm not doing it again."

"Okay," Marissa said quietly.

Ryan nodded, then pointed the car toward home.

Seth and Ryan were having breakfast. Both grim and beaten down by the events of the previous night.

"I have no idea what to do," Seth said, gulping coffee. "I've never had a choice before. I've only had rejection. What do I do?"

"You're asking the wrong person," Ryan said. He refilled his coffee cup, then poured what was left in the pot into Seth's mug. "I'm through with women."

"Why? What happened?" Seth asked.

"Marissa got drunk. And we got pulled over by the cops."

"That Marissa sure does make life interesting," Seth said, giving Ryan an encouraging chuck on the shoulder.

Sandy wandered into the kitchen in a pair of pajama bottoms and a T-shirt. "What's so interesting?" he asked sleepily, just catching the end of their conversation. He scowled at the empty coffeepot, then set another pot to brewing.

"Marissa and I had a fight," Ryan said.

Sandy nodded. "Well, give it a couple days, I'm sure it'll blow over."

"Nah, I have to see her today. She's starting at her therapist's this morning, and I told her I'd go with her."

"You could," Sandy said, sitting down at the table next to the boys. "Or you could not."

"What do you mean?"

"Marissa has parents. And you have us. You don't need to take care of everything anymore. You could just — take it easy."

Ryan wasn't sure what to think — what Sandy was saying sounded too good to be true. He had always been the one to fix everything. Could he really just let go? He'd never considered the possibility. He glanced around the kitchen. At Sandy. At Seth. At Kirsten who'd just wandered in looking for coffee. A small smile played around his lips. Then he got up, heading toward the living room. The Cohens followed curiously.

Ryan picked up a Christmas stocking. Seth had given it to him, explaining that everyone in the family had one to hang over the fireplace. Ryan had resisted, but now he picked up the stocking with "Ryan" spelled out in black iron-on letters and moved toward the fireplace.

"I already put the hook up . . . just in case," Seth said. Ryan smiled at him, and as the Cohens watched, he hung his stocking next to theirs.

23

Marissa sat on a chair outside her therapist's office. She had pulled her knees up to her chest and was hugging them. It looked like she was trying to disappear, and honestly, she was. There was something so humiliating about being forced into therapy. It was like broadcasting to the world that she was so messed up she couldn't even handle her own mind.

Seated across from her was a boy whom, if Marissa hadn't been so freaked out, she would have classified as a hottie. He had dark hair and a brooding expression, and was completely absorbed in a book, *The Theory of the Working Class* by Thorsen Veblen.

Marissa studied him. He didn't look crazy. Then again, neither did she. And obviously he wouldn't be there if he wasn't completely messed up. Then again —

"Hi," he said, catching her looking at him.

Marissa blushed and looked down, resting her

forehead against her knees. But that didn't deter him.

"It's not as bad as you think," he said in a conspiratorial voice. "Dr. Milano is actually pretty cool."

"Right," Marissa said sarcastically.

"Of course, you can tell him anything you want. You know, if you want to keep secrets, there's no way he'll ever know."

Marissa lifted her head and looked him straight in the face. "You want me to lie to my therapist?" she asked, starting to smile.

The hottie lifted his hands in a gesture of total innocence. "I would never advocate lying," he said, and Marissa laughed.

"I'm Oliver," the boy said.

Marissa straightened out in her seat, uncurling herself from the protective position she'd been in, and gave him her best smile. "I'm Marissa."

The door to the office opened and a receptionist gestured for Marissa that it was her turn.

"Nice meeting you, Marissa," Oliver said.

"Will I see you next week?" Marissa asked.

"I certainly hope so," he answered, and with one last toss of her hair, Marissa steeled her nerves and went in to face her therapist.

Dr. Milano was young and pudgy, with an earnest expression that made Marissa assume he was too innocent to ever understand what she was going through. People who smiled so openly and pumped your hand hard when they shook it could never understand what it's like to have parents like hers, live in a town as presumptuous as Newport Beach, deal with the ultrasophisticated kids who went to Harbor. But when Marissa politely informed him of this, he just laughed.

"Are you kidding? I grew up in New York on the Upper East Side. I went to high school with the Saudi crown prince. Nothing you can say is going to shock me."

"I hate my mother." Saying it aloud was actually pretty shocking to Marissa herself, but Dr. Milano just waved his hand around dismissively.

"Oldest story in the book. What did she do to you? Take away your car? Steal from your trust fund?"

"She tried to have me locked up in a mental institution."

"Yeah, that's pretty bad. I can see why you'd be mad about that."

"That's not even all of it," Marissa said, and surprised herself a second time by bursting into tears. Dr. Milano passed her a box of Kleenex and leaned forward, waiting patiently for her to catch her breath to go on. "She sent my father away. She is trying to get rid of everybody. She ruined our family."

"Why did she send your father away?"

"He embarrassed her. He lost his job and went bankrupt, and she couldn't take how it looked."

"And she tried to send you away once before and didn't succeed. What do you think will happen if you embarrass her now?"

Marissa snuffled into a tissue and thought about it. Now that she was living with Jimmy, Julie didn't have too much power over her anymore. So why was she still so afraid of displeasing her?

"I think," Marissa said slowly, "that maybe I don't hate her, but I'm afraid of her."

"Why is that?"

"I don't know," Marissa said, and Dr. Milano smiled, leaning back in his chair and propping his feet comfortably against the edge of the coffee table. "Maybe that's something we can figure out in here together. What do you think?"

"That might be okay," Marissa said. She rubbed her palms over her eyes to get rid of the last few tears, then gave the doctor a tentative smile in return.

"Good," he said. "Let's get to work."

So three times a week, Marissa would duck out of her after-school activities a little early and head down to Dr. Milano's office. It actually did make her feel better, having someone she could say anything she wanted to, rant and swear and cry, spill all her family's deepest, darkest secrets, with no consequences. And every time she arrived, Oliver was sitting in the waiting room. He was funny and smart, and dark in a different way than Ryan. With Ryan, Marissa always felt like there were things she couldn't mention, parts of his life she'd be better off not knowing about. Oliver also had dealt with a lot of problems, but he talked about them freely, getting all his demons out in the sunlight, exorcising them that way.

Before long, Marissa found herself leaving school earlier and earlier so she could spend more time hanging out in the waiting room. Then they got into the habit of grabbing a cup of coffee after their sessions. They'd hole up on a couch at the little beatnik café down the street, and tell each other all the stuff they didn't tell their therapists — things about school and friends and sex that they'd be too embarrassed to discuss with an adult, even a therapist.

The one person who wasn't happy about Marissa and Oliver's friendship was Ryan. It seemed like every other sentence out of Marissa's mouth was about Oliver, and that she saw more of Oliver than she did of him. On top of that, Ryan hadn't quite forgiven Marissa for her behavior at Christmas. She'd told him she was working on it with her therapist, but she'd never said "I'm sorry," and for some reason, that really bugged him. It was as if she didn't understand that he could have been sent back to juvie if the cop had found the open bottle of scotch in the car. Instead of trying to make it up to him, Marissa was having coffee dates with some jerk from therapy? It made him mad.

Plus, the more she talked about Oliver and the things he did and said, the more it became clear to

Ryan that Oliver wanted something other than just friendship from Marissa. Ryan tried to discuss the idea that Oliver was in love with her, but Marissa would just shake her head and accuse Ryan of not trusting her.

"I do trust you," Ryan told her. "I just don't trust him."

But Marissa wouldn't listen. And neither would anyone else — even Seth. Ryan couldn't understand why no one else could see that Oliver was constantly trying to get Marissa alone, to separate her from her friends — especially from Ryan. The only person who noticed was Luke, but Marissa wasn't about to listen to anything he said, either.

"Why, Ryan?" she asked angrily. "Why don't you trust him?"

"He's obsessed with you —"

"He is not obsessed with me. But you? *Are* obsessed with him."

"He's in love with you!" Ryan exclaimed.

"He is not! God, Ryan, we have this same argument over and over again, I'm sick of it!"

"Oh, you're sick of it? How do you think I feel?" Ryan retorted. "I'm always having to rescue you from the messes you get into —"

"I don't need to be rescued!" Marissa shouted. "And more than that, I don't *want* your help."

"Oh, I guess you don't need me now that you have Oliver —"

"Oh my god. I can't do this anymore. I can't deal with you not trusting me. I think we should —"

Marissa faltered, afraid to say the words. But Ryan said them for her.

"You want to break up?"

Marissa nodded.

And without another word, Ryan turned and walked away.

Marissa stared after him. She wanted to call him back, but she couldn't, so instead she called Oliver.

"Hi," she said. "Can I come over?"

A short while later Marissa was sitting in Oliver's suite at the Four Seasons. A room service meal was spread out on the table between them and Oliver was lifting all the dish covers while talking non-stop.

"So, if we leave for L.A. after our massages, we can check into my parents' suite by two. Or we could go to Paris, how about it?"

"Oliver, I can't just go to Paris," Marissa began. The conversation felt weird, and she was starting to get uncomfortable.

"Why not? You've been saying that you want to get away from your mom. And you shouldn't be around Ryan now. This way it'll just be you and me . . . unless you don't want to hang out with me." Oliver sounded hurt.

"No, it's not that," Marissa said, quickly. "I just can't take off." She smiled nervously.

Oliver looked at her, then nodded and continued to talk, but Marissa wasn't listening. All she wanted to do was get out of there now. She wondered if she could find an excuse to get away, make a call, when

Oliver suddenly stood up and announced that he needed something from the other room.

Marissa grabbed her cell phone out of her purse and dialed Ryan's number. "Ryan. It's me. I'm at the hotel. I can't really talk. Oliver's — he's — you were right . . . about everything, and now I can't leave . . ."

"Hang up," said a voice behind her. Marissa turned slowly. Oliver was standing there. He had a gun.

"Marissa!" Ryan's voice echoed down the phone. "What's going on? Marissa!" But Oliver had shut the phone.

Ryan raced into the Cohens' kitchen where everyone had gathered for dinner. He grabbed Sandy's car keys and headed toward the door.

"Where do you think you're going?" Sandy asked.

"Marissa's in trouble. I'm just going to make sure she's okay," Ryan said.

"No, you're not. Give me the keys," Sandy said, blocking Ryan's way. Ryan stared at him in disbelief, but Sandy wasn't moving. He held out his hand. "Give me the keys," he said more forcefully. "I'll drive." Ryan stared at him in amazement then handed over the keys.

At the Four Seasons, Marissa was getting more and more panicky. Oliver wouldn't put the gun down. He kept raving on about how the gun was for him if Marissa decided to leave.

"Marissa, I'm in love with you. I always have been. How could you not know that? You're the one. You're the only one who gets me. The only thing in my life I really care about. If you leave, I won't have anything left to live for. So, you have to promise me you won't leave. Promise me!"

Just then there was a knock at the door. "Marissa!" Ryan cried.

"Ryan! He's got a gun!"

The door flew open as hotel security, Sandy, and Ryan burst in. Oliver swung round, to face them, holding the gun to his head.

"Oliver, put the gun down. *Please*," Ryan said. "Why would you want to do this? You're gonna hurt Marissa. The one person who cares about you the most. And I know you don't want to do that."

"You don't know anything about me," Oliver cried.

"I know more than I want to. I know what it's like to be abandoned by your parents. Your friends. To have no one in your life who believes in you. But I also know that if you put the gun down, you can have a second chance. But it's your life, it's your choice. You do what you want. I can't stop you."

For a moment no one moved. Then Oliver dropped the gun and began to sob.

Marissa ran into Ryan's arms. "I'm so sorry," she cried.

He held her, stroking her back. "It'll be okay," he said. But would it?

24

"So tonight's the Valentine's Day Singles' Gala to benefit the hospital . . . anyway, I wondered . . .," Seth looked at Ryan. He was floundering around, and Ryan wasn't giving him a clue. He tried again, "I mean, you're not gonna go, right? It's a singles event and you're not single."

"I dunno. I mean — we broke up. We haven't talked about it," Ryan finally said.

"Great! So I'm not going alone," Seth said, relieved.

"Why're you going? Didn't Anna break up with you because of you and Summer?"

"First of all, Anna didn't break up with me . . . okay, she did," Seth admitted. "Second of all, how Summer feels about me is . . . unclear."

The truth was, Anna *had* broken up with Seth and it *was* because of Summer. Anna and Seth should have been the perfect couple — they loved sailing and the same music, comic books, but the truth was that it always been about Summer for

Seth, so he tried including her. With disastrous results. The night of the final showdown with Oliver, Anna and Seth had been arguing — quietly, but arguing — about Seth's exact relationship with Summer. He maintained that they were just friends, but Anna knew better. She was supposed to be dating Seth so why were there three people in the relationship? The final straw had occurred when Ryan and Sandy returned to say that Marissa was okay. Seth's first reaction had been to call Summer to let her know. Anna had finally snapped.

Seth could still hear her words: "Look, I think you're great. But I'm not going to stick around acting like I'm your girlfriend, when I'm not. At least not anymore. I'll see you at school." And then she was gone.

Seth pulled out of his reverie and glanced at Ryan.

"What's the chance of us missing this dance?" Ryan asked.

"None," Seth said with a sigh. "None."

The Valentine's Day party was a typical Newport event — lots of tanned skin, jewelry, and money on display. Ryan was really starting to wish that he'd never come. He looked around the room. No, he really didn't belong here. Just then Marissa approached him, a strangely shy expression on her face. She stopped in front of him, smiling uncertainly. They were like strangers.

"Can we just start over?" she finally asked.

"Start over?" Ryan asked.

"I'm Marissa. You go to Harbor, right?" She extended her hand.

Ryan looked from her hand to her face. Finally he spoke, "I know what you're trying to do. And I — I can't . . . I'm sorry."

He gave her one last searching look. Then headed for the door, leaving a totally crushed Marissa staring at his back.

An hour later. Marissa had arrived at the party with her dad, and she had no way to get home until he was ready to leave. So she sat alone at a table on the edge of the ballroom, her head buried in her hands so no one could see the tears dripping down her face.

All she wanted was to be left alone, but someone stopped by her table, and when she looked up, Sandy Cohen was standing next to her, his hand resting on the back of the empty chair across from her.

"Mind if I sit down for a minute?" he asked, and Marissa shook her head, offering up a weak smile.

Sandy sat and looked at the thin, miserable girl for a minute, then jumped right in.

"Here's the thing about Ryan —"

Oh god, this was a nightmare. She couldn't bear it. She had to stop him. "I'm not — this isn't — I'm fine —" she stammered, but Sandy wasn't buying it for a second.

"The thing about Ryan is when things get tough, everybody in his life abandons him."

"But I didn't," Marissa said, tears welling up in her eyes. "He thinks I did, but I didn't. I wouldn't."

"Then show him you didn't," Sandy said, offering Marissa a napkin. "Show him that you're not gonna give up on him."

Marissa wiped her eyes. "He wants me to leave him alone."

"Only because he expects you to. Love isn't easy, but you gotta hang in there. Because it's worth it."

Marissa nodded, and Sandy stood. "You guys have been through too much to quit now."

Ryan managed to hold it together until he got outside. But as soon as the heavy oak doors leading out of the club had banged shut behind him, he let out a roar of anger and slammed his fist into the side of the building.

"Goddamn it!" he shouted, trying to shake the pain out of his hand.

One of the caterers who'd been sitting on the steps taking a break turned around to see what all the noise was about.

"Ryan?" Theresa said, looking surprised.

"Theresa! Are you — are you working here?"

"I figured, what better use of my life than to serve paté to a bunch of rich people."

Ryan grinned, cradling his hurt hand. Theresa walked up to him and gently took it in hers to examine it.

"What happened?"

"I punched a wall."

Theresa let out a snort. "Nice to know you haven't changed. Come on, let's go get this wrapped up."

Ryan looked back at the doors to the party. "You don't need to get back to work?"

"They can live without me for an hour," she said. "Let's go."

Ryan hesitated, half expecting Marissa to come running out after him, sorry about the fight and wanting to make up. If she did that, he would take her back in a heartbeat. But she didn't come out, so he draped his good arm over Theresa's shoulders, and off they went.

When Marissa arrived at the pool house, she had already worked out exactly what she'd say. First she'd apologize for not believing Ryan. She'd beg him to forgive her. And then, after he'd forgiven her and they were back together, she'd tell him she loved him. And who knows, she might even *show* him.

She'd been thinking about it a lot lately and maybe it was time for her and Ryan to have sex. Kissing him made her feel deliriously happy, but she was definitely feeling an itch to move things forward. And although she had no real basis of comparison, on TV shows they always were saying that "makeup sex" was especially good, so what better moment for their first time?

She had a condom in her purse that Summer had given her before she'd slept with Luke. She'd been carrying it around half as a joke, and partly because she didn't know that she could trust herself to say no when she was with Ryan. Came in handy, now that she was planning to say yes. She assumed that the condom would still be good after six months — she wasn't sure and couldn't remember from sex ed in health class if they had expiration dates. Well, maybe Ryan would know. Besides, he might have had a stash of them — he was a boy, after all.

She got to the Cohens' and walked over to the pool house and put her hand on the door. She felt a rush of excitement and nerves wash over her and took a deep breath before pushing open the door. But she needn't have gotten so worked up: Nobody was there.

When they left the party, Ryan didn't feel like going back to the Cohens', so they decided to take a walk, and Theresa pointed the car toward the ocean. The sky was overcast, so the beach was practically deserted, just a couple of boys throwing sticks for a giant yellow Lab, and a lone surfer bobbing on the waves.

They took off their shoes and walked along the water's edge, trying to get over the awkwardness of seeing each other after so long apart.

"Ryan Atwood," Theresa said, breaking the silence. "Look at yourself. New clothes, new haircut, dating the homecoming queen."

Ryan let out an angry little bark of laughter, and Theresa grinned wryly. "*Was* dating?"

Ryan shrugged. "I guess. I dunno."

But Theresa had known him too long to be fooled by his cavalier attitude. She bumped her hip against his and threaded her arm around his waist. Ryan smiled, resting against her for just a second, then tossed his arm around her shoulders as they continued down the beach.

"Do you ever think about coming home?" Theresa asked quietly.

"I don't have a home," he said, kicking at a piece of driftwood.

"You know what I mean," Theresa prodded, and Ryan sighed, throwing his head back to look at the wide expanse of gray sky.

"Sometimes. More lately." He looked at Theresa, the half smile playing on her lips when he admitted this, and gave her a nudge. "You ever think about leaving?"

"Oh yeah. All the time. But I don't know how." She balled up her fists in frustration. "My mom got laid off last month. Arturo got arrested. I don't have a lot of options."

"And when you took this particular catering job . . ." Ryan started, and Theresa turned to face him.

"I needed the money, and . . . I was hoping to run into you. Home's lonely these days."

Ryan knew exactly how she felt. So without another word, he lowered his face to hers in a kiss that managed to make their loneliness recede, at least for a little while.

25

Summer was lying on her bed watching TV when someone knocked on the door.

"I'm busy. Studying. Naked," she called out in annoyance.

"Is that supposed to keep me away?" Seth called from outside.

"Cohen?" Summer sprang up and opened the door. "You're at my house."

Seth walked into the room and began to look around, pausing to pick up a small plastic horse sitting on Summer's bedside table.

"What are you doing here?" Summer asked, snatching the pony out of Seth's hand.

"Okay, before you give me the boot, give me a second. To explain. It's not so much that since Anna and I broke up that *now* I'm choosing you. It's . . . well . . . the whole reason we broke up is 'cause — for me —" Seth paused, taking a deep breath. This was hard. "Summer, it's *always* been you. Always. Try as I did to fight it. Deny it. But you're undeniable."

Almost before he'd finished speaking, Summer grabbed him and kissed him hard, pushing him down on the bed. Before Seth could even register what was happening, she was tearing at his clothes.

"Cohen — do you happen to have — you know — a — you know," Summer suddenly asked.

Seth nodded mutely and began to speak, but Summer clamped her hand over his mouth. "Well, you're about to get lucky," she said.

A half an hour later, Seth was back outside, walking home.

"Well, *that* didn't go well," he muttered to himself. Who knew that sex would be so difficult? It was one thing to make out with a girl, but sex was a whole different ball game. There were too many limbs, for one thing. Where was he supposed to put his arms? And her legs were just in the way. He couldn't see how he was supposed to have sex with a girl who had legs. Although he guessed people had done it before. He'd talk to Ryan about it.

"That sounds . . . weird," Ryan said, after Seth had described it all to him. Theresa had to get back to her catering job, so Ryan came back to the Cohens' and was aimlessly flipping through the channels on the TV, unable to focus on any one program, but desperate to be distracted enough to keep from thinking about his own troubles. Hearing about Seth's sexual conquests was as good a distraction as any.

"It was weird!" Seth agreed. "Awkward. Like, I've been dreaming of this my entire life, and then we do it, and I sucked. I was like a fish flopping around on dry land. I was Nemo, Ryan, and I just wanted to go home."

"Maybe Summer didn't notice. It's different for girls," Ryan said, grasping at straws.

"Oh, right, she didn't notice the bad fish sex. What am I going to do?"

"Well, for starters, I wouldn't refer to it as fish sex ever again."

"Done," Seth said, nodding. "What next?"

Ryan looked at Seth and smiled. "Do it again. Only better this time."

"Thanks," Seth said. "You've been a big help."

Ryan pulled Theresa close to him, wrapping his arms tight around her and running his hands over her silky skin. They were lying in Theresa's bed in her rented room at the Mermaid Inn, taking comfort in the familiar feeling of each other's bodies. Things felt right with Theresa, easy and familiar — even when they made love. They had picked up with each other right where they left off, as if nothing had changed. As if they were back in high school . . . back to being boyfriend and girlfriend.

But things had changed. Ryan was in love with someone else now. But Marissa had deserted him, the exact same way his mom and his dad and everyone else he had ever loved in his life had deserted him. Love brought you nothing but trouble and pain, and he was through with it.

So even though he didn't love Theresa, and she didn't love him, she was consistently a good thing for him. There weren't any mad ups and downs with her. Plus Theresa was there, she was warm and soft and comfortable, and for now, he'd take that over love.

26

Seth was lying on his bed, talking to Captain Oats. "Not to rub it in, but I think Summer's horse was your type . . . I blew it for both of us, buddy." He paused. How pathetic was he, talking to a toy horse?

Suddenly there was a knock at the door and Summer entered the room. Seth scrambled to his feet, trying to hide the plastic toy.

"Summer. What's up?" he asked, trying to be nonchalant.

Summer paused for a minute then launched into her speech. "When we had sex the other night — you weren't the only virgin in the room."

Seth stared at her, stunned. "Someone else was in the room?" he finally asked, not sure what he was hearing.

"Me, idiot. I'm a virgin. Was a virgin."

"Why didn't you tell me . . .?"

"I don't know. I had a reputation to uphold. And

I figured you'd think less of me or something . . ." Summer's words trailed off.

"No. Not at all. But I'm stunned. This was a huge moment in our lives and we just blew past it. It's a big deal."

"It should have been special," Summer said, quietly.

"Well, why don't we just slow things down? Start from the beginning?" Seth asked, walking to the record player and putting on some music. As the song began to play softly, he held out his hands, gesturing that they should dance.

Summer smiled, embarrassed, but she moved toward him, putting her arms around him and resting her head against his chest.

"Hey. I'm really sweeping you off your feet, huh?" Seth asked.

"The sad part is," Summer replied, lifting her face to look at him, "you kind of are . . ."

Luke, meanwhile, had been thinking about what happened at the Valentine's Day party. Marissa had looked so upset, that he was worried and decided the best thing to do was to go find her and make sure she was all right.

She wasn't at Jimmy's apartment when he stopped by, and after checking the beach and the galleria and all the other places where he knew she liked to hang out, he decided that the one place left to look for her was Julie Cooper's house, just in case she was staying at her mom's.

Luke realized the second that Julie opened the door Marissa wasn't there.

"I don't know where she is," Julie said ruefully. "She doesn't tell me much of anything anymore."

"I'm sure she'll stop being mad," Luke said awkwardly, not sure how else to comfort her. "I mean, she forgave me."

"Well, I hope so," Julie said, starting to close the door, but Luke wasn't finished talking. "You've always been the coolest mom, and whenever we play Ultimatum —"

"What's Ultimatum?" Julie asked.

"Where you rate who you'd rather do. Of all your friends' moms —"

"That's a game?"

"Uh-huh. And you always won."

"Really?" Julie asked. She and Caleb had had a fight, so she'd been working her way through a bottle of wine when Luke stopped by, and suddenly she realized just how attractive her daughter's ex-boyfriend really was.

"Really," Luke affirmed. "Mrs. Cooper, you're totally hot."

Julie smiled, and before she knew what she was doing, she leaned forward and pressed her lips against his. It was the sweetest, most tender kiss Luke had ever felt, and as Julie started to pull away, Luke pressed forward, keeping the kiss going for as long as he could. At last they broke away, breathless, and Julie could feel her heart hammering in her chest, thudding harder than it ever did when she kissed Caleb Nichol. Before she had time to talk herself out of it, Julie grabbed Luke's hand and pulled him inside, shutting the door behind them with a bang.

27

For the next few weeks, things settled into a sort of routine. Marissa was taking Sandy's advice very much to heart. Even though she was used to getting what she wanted, she also knew she couldn't compete with someone Ryan had known his whole life. So she decided to befriend Theresa, or at least be really nice to her. Theresa seemed a little taken aback by the attention, but Marissa figured this was the best way to show Ryan she wasn't giving up on him. Besides, Ryan was only able to see Theresa in the evenings when she wasn't working, which gave Marissa the entire school day to work on winning him back.

Whenever Marissa saw Summer sitting at lunch with Seth and Ryan, she would go over and put her tray down next to them, chatting and laughing as though her heart wasn't shattered in a million pieces. And the more normal she acted, the more Ryan warmed up. It wasn't as good as getting back together, but at least they were able to start hanging out a little again.

Ryan was totally relieved that Marissa was calming down, too. For a while there, any time he spotted her, she was either crying or silently staring at him with red-rimmed eyes. It made him feel terrible. Marissa had enough unhappiness in her life without him making things worse. But now she was starting to get back to her old self. It was weird, but now that they were spending time together again, it kind of made him miss her more. Maybe it was because they were never alone together — they only saw each other when Seth and Summer were around. But also, seeing her laughing and cracking jokes reminded Ryan of why he had fallen in love with her to begin with.

But as much as he would have liked to go back to the way things had been, he didn't know how. The real truth was that nothing could erase the fight they had had, that he couldn't trust her. And while he was more than willing to forgive her, he simply couldn't make himself forget.

Seth, on the other hand, was feeling pretty happy. He was having lunch with Summer and Anna — his girlfriend and his best friend. He couldn't imagine how it could get better. Well, that wasn't quite true.

Although they'd all agreed to stay friends, something had definitely changed in their relationship. Anna didn't hang out with him as much as she used to, even when Summer wasn't around, and when they were together, she was more subdued, not as quick to laugh or tease him. Seth really missed that, but he didn't know how to fix it, either.

"I'm leaving," Anna said, rising from the table where she'd been eating lunch with Seth and Summer.

"To get dessert?" Seth asked, but Anna shook her head.

"To go back to Pittsburgh."

Seth and Summer looked at each other in shock. "What?!"

"I'm gonna live with my aunt and uncle. I've just kind of . . . had enough of Newport," Anna said, and she tossed her coffee cup in the trash and left Seth and Summer staring wide-eyed after her.

All day long Seth felt terrible. Had he driven Anna away? He really did like her a lot. And while he wouldn't give up what he had with Summer for the world, the last thing he wanted was to hurt Anna so much she'd leave the state of California! He kept trying to talk to her, but he couldn't get a second alone with her. Finally, after school, he cornered her just as she was about to get into her car.

"Hey, Anna, can I talk to you for a minute?" he asked, and Anna nodded, one hand on the door of her car, as if she might flee at any moment.

"What's up?" she asked.

"Did you see the Lakers won?"

Anna cracked a smile. "Oh, did they?"

"Yeah. They did," Seth continued. "There was something else I wanted to ask you — what was it? Oh yeah . . . You're leaving?! Why the hell are you leaving?!!!"

"Seth," Anna said, opening her car door, "it's complicated. . . ."

But Seth wouldn't let her off the hook. "Give me one reason. There's got to be one major overriding reason."

Anna thought for a second. "I miss seasons. Fall foliage. Snow. The first day of spring."

"Seasons." She was lying! Seth knew it. It was his fault. But Anna was still talking.

"I miss my dog, Swifty, who we left with my aunt and uncle. The Jimmy Stewart museum. Peanut butter cup pie at Dingbats. The vinyl selection at Record Village. A couple frames at the Arsenal Bowling Alley. The jukebox at Gooski's. Sundays at Superflea flea market."

She finished and looked at Seth so openly that before he could stop himself, he had to ask.

"So you're not leaving because of me?"

Anna touched his arm. "I'm leaving because I need to leave. I'm lonely, Seth. I thought I could make this my home, but I can't. So I gotta go home."

And with that, she got in her car and drove away, taking a bit of Seth's heart along with her.

Ryan knew that Seth was missing Anna, and he felt bad about it, but he had problems of his own. Theresa was no closer to figuring out what she was going to do, and she was growing more and more frustrated with her situation with each passing day. And every time Ryan offered to help her, she grew angry, saying she wasn't some helpless Newport chick and could take care of herself. But Ryan knew there was more to it than that: Theresa told him that before she left Chino, she had been dating Eddie, a kid from the old neighborhood. Eddie was bad news, as far as Ryan was concerned. He didn't know how serious it was between the two of them, or if Eddie was part of the reason Theresa had come to Newport, but he knew that whatever it was, it wasn't good.

That evening, the Cohens were hosting a party for Caleb, who was being named Man of the Year. Caleb had been driving Kirsten crazy with his requests, but by the time the party got under way, everything was perfect. White lights twinkled in the trees, waiters passed through the crowd carrying trays of hors d'oeuvres, and everyone who was anyone was there. Ryan was talking to Summer when her eyes suddenly widened. Following her gaze, Ryan caught sight of Theresa but this wasn't the Theresa he was used to. . . . She looked fabulous. She was wearing a new dress and her hair and makeup were perfect. Marissa stood behind her, surveying the crowd. She smiled as Ryan and Summer walked up to them.

"Hey. You look . . . wow," was all Ryan could manage.

Theresa smiled. "I had some help."

Ryan looked at Marissa and smiled gratefully, then he took Theresa's arm and they moved away.

"Talk about *Extreme Makover*," said Summer. "So. What? Is this, like, some plan — bring Pretty Woman to the polo grounds so she gets that she doesn't fit in?"

Marissa shook her head.

"Sorry. I've just seen that movie four hundred times."

"This was just me . . . trying to help," Marissa said, looking at Ryan and Theresa.

Caleb gestured for the crowd to quiet down as he began to speak. Ryan was searching the crowd for Seth. Anna had slipped into the party a few minutes earlier, and given him a letter for Seth. She said she couldn't stick around to talk to him herself, and asked Ryan to deliver the letter for her. He promised that he would, but he was distracted by the sight of someone he never expected to see: Theresa's fiancé, Eddie. Ryan had known Eddie back in Chino and considered him bad news. While he and Theresa hadn't discussed it, he couldn't help wondering if part of the reason she'd come to Newport was to get away from Eddie. She never said anything, but then she never talked about him at all. Now, Eddie was standing behind her, whispering urgently. Theresa turned, stunned.

"What are you doing here?" she asked.

"Taking you home. So we can figure this out," he replied.

"I'm not going anywhere," Theresa replied. People were starting to look, turning around to see what was going on.

Ryan moved quickly toward Eddie. "Hey, let's take this somewhere else," he urged.

"Dude. You're lucky I don't kick your —" Eddie began, then stopped. "I'm leaving. Theresa's coming with me. Enjoy your party." He started to take Theresa's arm, but she shook him off. Ryan grabbed Eddie, who spun around and clocked Ryan right in the face. Everything stopped for a moment and everyone stared. Eddie went for Ryan again, but this time, Ryan was ready and he swung back, giving Eddie as good as he got. Ryan and Eddie continued to shove each other, as guests scrambled to get out of the way. Eddie lowered his shoulder, driving into Ryan, and pushing him back into a table. They continued to trade punches, until the flash from a reporter's camera distracted Ryan. It was the opportunity Eddie needed. He took one mighty swing, leveling Ryan, who stumbled backward and fell into the pool.

Luke lunged forward and grabbed Eddie, wrapping him in a bear hug. Sandy and Jimmy joined him in controlling the still-raging Eddie.

"Why don't you leave before the cops get here?" Sandy advised him.

Eddie broke free, but realized that he was outnumbered. He turned back to face Ryan, who was treading water in the pool. "You're dead," he warned. "Don't ever come back home, kid!" With that parting shot, he stormed out of the backyard.

Silence settled over the crowd, until someone tittered nervously. Seth reached down and helped Ryan out of the pool.

Needless to say, the party ended quickly after that. Inside the house, Ryan was sitting on the couch, holding an ice pack to his face.

"It's gonna be a shiner, but they look good on you," Sandy assured him.

"Yeah. Thanks," Ryan said, wincing.

Kirsten was handing tissues to Theresa. "I'm so sorry. About everything," Theresa kept saying.

"What are you gonna do now?" Ryan asked her.

"I need to call Eddie. Try and straighten everything out," Theresa said.

"It'll be okay," Ryan reassured her. Theresa smiled and gave him a kiss on the forehead before turning and walking out of the house.

When they entered the room where everyone else was sitting, Seth was still complaining that he couldn't believe that Anna hadn't shown up. Suddenly Ryan remembered the letter in his coat. He reached into the pocket and pulled out the sopping wet letter.

"You're just giving me this now?!" Seth exclaimed.

"I was a little distracted," Ryan replied.

"I can't read it. The ink is all smudged," Seth

said, holding the letter out to Summer and pointing at it. "Is that a v — or a q — or . . ." He pulled the letter back. "There, right after it says 'I love you' what is that? Azerbaijan? Aztec?"

"What do you care what it says?" Summer asked, angrily.

"You're right. The fact that she wrote me a letter *says* everything She couldn't say good-bye. She's leaving 'cause of me. I've got to stop her!"

"What is going on?" Summer asked, getting even angrier, if that was possible.

"Summer, she's my friend. I don't want her to leave."

"Then go. Stop her," Summer said, turning away. Which was just what Seth planned to do. One small problem: He'd had too much to drink and couldn't drive himself so . . . Ryan reluctantly agreed to.

In the car, Seth was now making Ryan crazy.

"C'mon, man. Her flight leaves soon," he urged.

"I'm doing seventy-five in a sixty-five," Ryan replied.

"Everyone knows eighty is the new seventy-five," Seth responded.

Ryan just gave him a look.

"And what's with this music?" Seth asked, reaching for the radio.

"Do not insult Journey," Ryan said, giving him another glare that forced Seth to sit back quietly for the rest of the ride.

Finally, they reached the airport. Before the car even stopped moving, Seth was out the door and running through the terminal. There! Just ahead of him! He could see Anna's blond head and her sock monkey sticking out of her backpack. She was already at security.

"Anna! Wait! Stop!" he cried.

Anna turned around. She stared, then said something to the security guard and came to meet him.

"Seth? What are you doing here —?"

"Okay, maybe it's the champagne talking, but I'm just going to say it. . . . Don't leave because of me."

"*What*? Seth, you're an amazing guy. A little self-absorbed maybe. But great." She paused and shrugged. "But if our relationship taught me anything? We don't really have any chemistry. I'm leaving 'cause I need to leave. I thought I could make this my home. But . . . I can't. Thanks for coming. Thanks for saying good-bye." And with that, she turned and headed back through the security barrier and out of Seth's life.

The doorbell at Jimmy's apartment rang. Marissa opened the door to find Theresa there, holding her dress.

"I'm sorry. I won't have time to get it dry-cleaned . . . before I go."

"What do you mean?" Marissa asked.

"I've been . . . fooling myself. To think it was

gonna be easy. I've made a mess of everything. I've got this whole life I've got to figure out . . . and so does Ryan. Take care of him. I'll see you." She handed Marissa the dress, then walked away.

A short while later, Ryan and Seth pulled into the parking lot of the Mermaid Inn. Ryan wanted to make sure that Theresa was okay, but when he got to her room it was empty. A maid was changing the sheets. The room was clean. There was no sign that Theresa had ever been there.

Later that night, Seth and Ryan were sitting on the Newport Pier, eating pizza and watching the lights on the ships moving through the water.

"What if the girl I'm really s'posed to be with went back to Pittsburgh?" Seth said.

"What if she went back to Chino?" Ryan answered.

"Why would Anna go to Chino?" Seth said, then gave Ryan a crooked smile. "Kidding."

"At least we've got each other," Ryan said.

"Actually? I've got Summer. But I can carve out a little Seth-Ryan time." He grinned.

"What time is it?" Ryan asked, glancing down at his watch — but it wasn't there. "Oh god," he groaned, realizing.

"What?" Seth asked.

"I left my watch at the hotel." Ryan rolled his eyes — he didn't want to go back there ever, but Seth patted him on the back.

"Come on. I'll help you look for it."

And the two boys got up from the pier and headed back toward the Mermaid Inn.

"This is actually a good time for you," Seth told Ryan, as they pulled into the parking lot of the hotel.

Ryan shot Seth a look, but Seth continued blithely on. "I'm serious. Not having a girlfriend is the best thing that could happen to you. This is Clean-Slate Ryan. No entanglements with soon-to-be-married past lovers or pill-popping manic depressives."

"I do have a clean slate," Ryan agreed, not exactly perking up, but at least willing to listen. Seth noticed the good sign and kept building his case.

"Since day one in Newport, you've had nothing but lady drama. You deserve a break! And you're going to get it. No more punches to be thrown, no more hearts to be broken — nothing to do but hang out with me, having fun and being free."

"That does sound kind of good," Ryan said.

Seth gave him an affectionate punch on the arm. "Plus, you now have time to finally finish reading *Kavalier and Clay*."

"You and that book!" Ryan said.

But Seth was serious. "It's the story of two young men who are more like brothers. Who are always there for each other. Just like us."

"You're right," Ryan said. "I'll read it."

"Good," Seth told him, "'cause you'll need

something to do while I'm off having sex with Summer."

They reached the hotel and found the watch without too much difficulty. But as they were leaving, a movement caught Ryan's eye — it was Luke, knocking on the door of one of the rooms.

"What's he doing here?" Ryan asked Seth, pointing.

Seth cupped his hands around his mouth, ready to yell up to Luke, when the hotel room door opened. Julie Cooper was standing in the doorway!!

Seth and Ryan ducked down behind a car, watching as Luke and Marissa's mom kissed. Then Julie pulled Luke into the hotel room, shutting the door behind them, and Seth and Ryan looked at each other, horrified.

"Oh my god," Seth breathed. "Did you see that?"

Ryan nodded, unable to speak.

"What are we going to tell Marissa?" Seth asked, and Ryan found his voice.

"Nothing."

28

The next morning, Ryan caught up with Luke outside of their biology lab. The pair had been on pretty good terms recently. But what he'd seen last night changed everything. If Marissa found out that Luke was sleeping with her mom, well, Ryan wasn't sure what she'd do, but he knew that it wouldn't be good.

"Hey, man," Luke said, smiling at Ryan. He started to go into the classroom, but Ryan caught his sleeve, stopping him. "What's up?"

"Nothing," Ryan said, then dropped his voice. "Just wondering if you banged Julie Cooper again this morning."

Luke took a step backward, dropping his biology book. He bent down to pick it up, trying to think up an answer for Ryan that wouldn't be totally incriminating. "How did you —?" he asked, and Ryan grimaced.

"I saw you guys at the Mermaid Inn last night."

"I know what it looked like, but you don't understand. I'm really into her. We have a connection."

Ryan slammed his fist against the side of a

locker and leaned in to threaten Luke. "What were you thinking? If Marissa finds out —"

"She won't," Luke said, shaking his head. "We're being careful."

"She's going to find out. Unless you end it now."

"I can't," Luke pleaded.

"You have to."

Luke promised Ryan he would break it off with Julie that evening. On the off chance that Marissa would decide that that was the night she needed to stop by her mom's house to pick up more clothes or something, Ryan decided the best thing to do would be to ask her to go see a movie or something while Luke was with Julie.

"Just the two of us?" Marissa asked, surprised.

"Well, Seth and Summer already have tickets to see Bright Eyes, so instead of just hanging around the house all night, I thought it might be fun if we did something."

Marissa searched Ryan's face for a catch. He didn't come out and say that he wanted to get together, but this could be a first step. Then again — what about Theresa? Seth had told Summer that Theresa was back in Chino for good, but Marissa wasn't sure what that meant in the long run. Still, it was the first time in a long time that it had been just the two of them.

"Fun?" she repeated, teasing him. "You never think anything's fun."

"People change," Ryan said. His smile made Marissa's heart leap. "Besides, we're going to be living in the same town, going to the same school for a while. And we're friends, right? So, we need to get used to doing things together."

"That's true," Marissa said. "So — what movie do you want to see?"

They chose something innocuous and fun that wouldn't bring up any sort of issues they both would rather not discuss. The way a romance might. Afterward they went to get some ice cream. Marissa ordered a vanilla shake, and Ryan chose a peanut butter sundae. They sat on a little bench looking out over the ocean to eat.

"This is good," Ryan said. He took another bite of his sundae and smiled at her.

"Mine's good, too," Marissa said, toasting him with her shake, and Ryan laughed.

"No, I meant us hanging out together is good."

"Yeah," Marissa said softly. She looked out at the ocean, the waves crashing on the dark shore. "It is."

Luke was not having a very good night. Usually he had to make plans far in advance to see Julie Cooper — she was scared to death that people would find out and talk. She had already been the source of so much gossip because of Jimmy's and Marissa's antics that she was not eager to contribute any more grist to the rumor mill.

But Ryan had convinced Luke that what they were doing was wrong — he and Julie both realized it, deep down. But it was going to be hard to stop seeing her. And the hardest part of all was going to be saying the words to her. She wasn't home when he got to her house, so Luke parked his car down the block and waited until he saw her headlights pulling in.

He got out of his car and stealthily made his way to her driveway, making sure she was alone.

Julie gave a little jump when she saw him. "You startled me," she said in a soft, laughing voice, reaching for him, but Luke took a step back.

"Mrs. Cooper," he said, and the anguish in his voice made her stop, aware that something wasn't right.

"What is it, Luke?"

"I can't — we can't do this anymore."

Julie stared at him for a moment before she spoke. "Excuse me? You're breaking up with me?"

Luke nodded miserably, and Julie gave him a tight smile. "Fine. Bye."

"That's it?" Luke asked, his voice catching in his throat. He wasn't sure what he wanted from her, but it sure as hell wasn't this cold indifference.

"Yes, Luke, that's it," Julie told him, her voice as sharp as razor blades. "You don't get to break up with me, then go for one last spin in the sack."

"Oh . . . okay," Luke said. He could feel tears coming, so he turned and walked down the driveway as quickly as he could, determined not to let her see him cry.

When he reached the bottom of the drive, he turned to say good-bye, but Julie had already gone inside.

Luke could see a light on in the Cohens' pool house next door, so he decided he might as well go tell Ryan he'd gone through with it and salvage what little respect the guy might still have for him.

He knocked on the door, and waited until he heard Ryan say come in. Luke stepped inside — Ryan was sitting on the edge of the bed, taking off his shoes. He looked surprised to see the other boy standing there.

"Luke — hey — give me a minute —"

But Luke didn't have a minute. He still felt that tight, heavy feeling behind his eyes, like any second he might not be able to hold the tears back, and it seemed to him that the only thing that could possibly be more humiliating than crying in front of Julie Cooper would be crying in front of Ryan.

"I did it," he said, his voice coming out in a rush. "I'm done having sex with Julie Cooper."

As the words were coming out of his mouth, Luke had the unfamiliar sensation of time slowing down. In slow motion, he turned his head to see Marissa coming out of the bathroom, hearing every word he said. Luke felt like he ought to be able to somehow snatch the words back, reach out and deflect them before they reached Marissa's ears, but of course that was impossible. Marissa dropped the towel she was holding and headed toward the door, dazed.

"Wait —" Ryan stood up to try and stop her, and she whirled on him, furious.

"Is that why you asked me to go to the movies? To cover for him?"

"I didn't want you to find out this way," Ryan whispered, but Marissa just looked at him, heart-broken.

"I gotta go," she said.

She got to the door, and Luke stepped aside to let her pass. "Marissa, I'm sorry," he said, and Marissa reached up and slapped his face as hard as she could.

Marissa didn't know what to do. Her life was just this never-ending pile of crap — as soon as she thought she had the possibility of being happy, another thing would come along to ruin everything.

Not sure what else to do, she went home. A few minutes later, the door burst open and Ryan came in.

"I'm so sorry," he said, coming over to hug her.

"You knew and you didn't tell me," Marissa said. She turned away from him.

Ryan put his arms around her. "I was just trying to make sure you didn't get hurt again," he whispered into her hair. "I just couldn't stand to see you sadder than you already are."

Marissa leaned against him, taking comfort in his size and strength. "I hate Luke," she said.

"Everyone hates Luke," Ryan agreed, earning a smile from her.

"God, what am I going to say to my mother when I see her?"

Ryan lifted one shoulder. "Tell her you know.

Tell her that this makes you even, and that she can't tell you what to do ever again."

"Do you think that would work?"

"No," Ryan said, and they both burst out laughing.

"God, I'm so glad you're here," Marissa said.

"I am, too," Ryan said, and suddenly they were kissing again, pressing against each other urgently, using their lips and hands and bodies to erase the bad feeling of the evening, to silently communicate that they still loved each other, that they wanted to be together, that they were sorry for everything that had happened.

The kiss was a promise of better things to come. And after Ryan had reluctantly pulled himself away and gone home, Marissa got into bed and for the first night in a very long time, she fell asleep without even thinking about taking another drink.

Luke spent a sleepless night, working his way through half a case of beer and making some choices. He didn't see any way that he could stay in Newport Beach and still be happy. People at school were bound to find out about his affair, and now that the gossip about his dad had finally started to die down, Luke couldn't face being the object of derision again so soon. He pretty much had no friends left. And even though he knew in his heart it was wrong, he really was head over heels in love with Julie Cooper.

There was no way she'd stay with him now, though, not once she knew people had discovered their secret. Plus she didn't seem like the kind of woman who was too free with second chances — look how she treated Marissa, and that was her own daughter.

No, there was no way Luke could face everybody now, so as the sun was starting to come up over the ocean, he pulled out his cell phone and called his dad at his new house in Portland, where he'd moved after the divorce had become final.

His dad's boyfriend answered the phone, and Luke hesitated, worried about how it would be to live in a house with two dads, but anything would be better than going back to Harbor. So when his dad got on the phone, Luke told him that he was taking him up on his standing offer to come live with him.

He would go home and pack, and tell his mom he was leaving. He'd like to apologize to Marissa, although he was pretty sure that she wouldn't agree to see him. But the one thing he did know was that there was no way he was leaving town without telling Julie Cooper that he loved her.

There was another party that evening — the opening of Jimmy and Sandy's new restaurant. It was the last place in the world Marissa wanted to be, but she couldn't stand to disappoint her dad by refusing to go. She'd just avoid her mom since, as far as she was concerned, the secret about her mom and Luke would go with her to the grave, and no way did she want her dad to catch on.

So she got in the car with him, buoyed only by the fact that Ryan would be there and that she and Ryan were together again, happily, perfectly in love, with all their fates aligned.

The party was small — friends and family, all gathered to sample the restaurant's menu and wish the new owners luck. It was Jimmy's big chance to start over in Newport, and he and Sandy had been hard at work for weeks. Now music was playing, and the guests were laughing and having a great time. It was a smash, by anyone's standards.

Ryan and Marissa stood a little apart from the rest of the guests, talking to Seth and Summer and watching the goings-on. Marissa had managed to avoid her mother completely, but she watched the way she stood with Caleb, his hand on the small of her back, and rolled her eyes.

She looked at Ryan, opening her mouth to say something sarcastic, but the music stopped abruptly as Caleb raised his hands for silence.

"I have an announcement to make," he called, and the crowd quieted down to hear what he had to say. "I hope everyone is enjoying themselves as much as I am," he said, "although my enjoyment of life these last few months is largely due to one special lady, Julie Cooper."

The guests applauded, and Marissa mimed sticking a finger down her throat to make herself throw up.

"And here, on this special night, I want to let Julie know just how special she is," he continued.

More applause, and then at the same time, Marissa and Ryan saw Luke stumble around the side of the restaurant. He was clearly drunk, and Ryan handed his glass to Seth, starting across the lawn to stop him from doing something that would embarrass them all.

"Hey, man, let's go," Ryan told him, putting a hand on his arm.

"I am going," Luke slurred, and Ryan reeled back from the waves of alcohol on his breath. "I'm going to Portland, but first I gotta do something."

Ryan shook his head. "Whatever it is, you don't want to do it," he said.

"I do," Luke insisted. "I gotta tell Julie Cooper that I love her."

"No —" Ryan started, but then Caleb was speaking again. He dropped to one knee and held out an enormous diamond to Julie. "Julie Cooper, will you marry me?"

"Yes," Julie squealed, and Ryan instinctively turned to look at Marissa. She had a hand covering her mouth, and her earlier parody of throwing up looked like it might actually happen any second now.

The guests were going wild, cheering and clapping, but over the noise, Ryan heard squealing tires. He turned just in time to see Luke's car peeling out of the parking lot and swerving out of sight down the road.

30

Luke raced down the street, drunkenly fighting to keep control of his truck as he swerved around corners, blinking tears out of his eyes. How could Julie do this to him? God, he hated her. He hated that she was marrying Caleb, that she let him break up with her, that she didn't love him back.

Maybe she actually did love him, he thought, and was just using Caleb to make him jealous. Maybe that was it. Luke dragged a sleeve over his eyes, wiping away his tears. He should call her and find out. She deserved another chance to be with him, if that's what she wanted. Maybe if he told her he loved her, she would change her mind about Caleb and come to Portland with him. And in any event, he still hadn't had a chance to say good-bye to her.

Luke pulled out his phone and snapped it open. He squinted at the numbers, which were blurring together in an alcoholic haze. He fumbled to dial her number and dropped the phone. Goddamn it. He took his hands off the wheel and bent down, groping around for it.

The last thing he remembered before the car crashed into a telephone pole and he blacked out was how happy he felt when his fingers finally touched the phone.

When Ryan and Marissa got to the hospital, Luke was still in the operating room. They had a seat on an uncomfortable couch in the visitors' area, and Marissa, exhausted, rested her head on Ryan's shoulder.

"When I saw him at the party tonight, I wished for something like this to happen," she said in a tiny voice.

"It's not your fault," Ryan said. He took her hand in his and held it tightly.

"God, I hope he's okay," she said, and Ryan was silent, hoping for the same thing.

What felt like hours later, a doctor came out and spoke to them.

"Your friend's pretty banged up, but he's going to be okay."

Ryan and Marissa looked at each other, smiles of relief crowding their faces. "Can we go see him?"

"His mother is in with him right now," the doctor told them, "but when she comes out you can go in."

Marissa was shocked at how small Luke looked, lying broken in the hospital bed. One leg was in a cast and there were bandages wrapped around his head. He opened his eyes when he heard the door open, and when he saw Ryan and Marissa standing there, tears coursed down his cheeks.

Marissa surprised herself by bursting into tears, too, and she sat down next to the bed, picking up his hand and clutching it.

"Are you okay?" Ryan asked in a husky voice.

"I'm so sorry," Luke said. There was a long pause as he struggled to find words. Ryan and Marissa waited, giving him time to collect himself.

"I didn't plan for it to happen," he told Marissa. "I never meant to hurt you. I'm gonna go live with my dad, but first, I have to know — can you forgive me?"

Marissa nodded. "I'll miss you," she said, and bent down to give him a gentle hug.

"So will I," Ryan said, and the two boys grinned at each other.

"Who would have thought?" Luke asked, and Ryan shrugged.

"Take care of yourself," he said, and Luke nodded, flashing his eyes at Marissa.

"Take care of her," he said softly.

"I will," Ryan said, and led Marissa from the room, with one last backward glance at their friend.

They were silent in the car heading back to the Cohens' house. Ryan drove, and Marissa sat as close to him as she could get. They both were feeling emotionally strung out, and the only salvation they could think of was each other. All Ryan wanted to do was to lie down with Marissa, shut his eyes, and hold her so tight he'd never let her go.

But when they got back to the Cohens' house, someone was waiting on the deck chairs outside of the pool house. It was Theresa.

Ryan felt weariness spread over him at the sight of her. He knew that this would be one more thing to upset Marissa and keep him from finally getting a little peace. But Theresa was his oldest friend, so he smiled and gave her a quick hug, keeping an eye on Marissa, who was looking at Theresa like she had three heads.

"Hi, Theresa," Ryan said. "What's up?"

Theresa glanced from Marissa to him, and then shrugged. "I'm pregnant."

31

Immediately after Theresa's bombshell, later that night, Marissa had beaten a hasty retreat, too wrecked from the past few days to get upset at this newest turn of events. Ryan had walked her down to her car to check in with her and make sure she was doing okay, but she simply told him she'd talk to him tomorrow, gave him a sweet kiss good night, then gotten in her car and driven home, where she stumbled right into bed and fell asleep before her head even hit the pillow.

At the Cohens', they were having a family conference. Theresa had eaten a little dinner and taken a hot shower, and was wrapped in Kirsten's robe, warming her hands around a cup of tea. Ryan sat next to her on the couch, unable to think of a single thing to say. Even Seth was uncharacteristically subdued, but that was fine, because Sandy was doing enough talking for all of them.

"You're sixteen," he told them, pacing back and forth. "You've got your whole lives ahead of you."

Theresa nodded. "I know," she whispered.

"Having a baby will ruin your life," Sandy said, and Kirsten put a hand on his arm.

"Sandy —" she said in a warning tone, but Sandy shook her off.

"It will ruin their lives! Ryan's only just gotten on his feet, he's doing well in school, making friends. He's got a great shot at getting into a good school, maybe even one of the Ivys. Do you know what having a baby will do to those plans?"

Ryan looked up. "Don't blame her. It's not her fault," he said sharply, and Sandy quickly nodded.

"I know, I'm not saying it is. But Theresa, you must have plans, too, plans that having a baby would interfere with."

"You're right," Theresa whispered, her eyes filling with tears.

Kirsten put an arm around her.

"I'll do whatever Theresa wants," Ryan said, and Theresa looked at him through watery eyes.

"The thing is, Ryan, I'm not even sure if it's yours."

Sandy and Kirsten exchanged a glance at this.

"You've been . . . seeing other people?" Kirsten asked delicately.

Theresa looked down, so Ryan spoke up. "Eddie."

"Does Eddie know about this?" Sandy asked, and Theresa shook her head.

"No. We broke up last month. I don't want to get back together with him, he's horrible," she said, sobbing. "But if we have a baby together . . . I just felt so alone, and I didn't know who else to come to."

"You can always come to us," Kirsten said, hugging the younger girl. "Ryan is our family, and you are always welcome here."

"My mom would help me raise it," Theresa said, drying her tears with a corner of the robe. "I just — even with her, I couldn't do it alone."

"I'm not going to let you down," Ryan said quietly. "No matter what you decide."

After everyone else had gone to bed, Sandy sat down on the couch next to Ryan.

"You know, this isn't your responsibility," he said in a quiet voice.

"Yes it is," Ryan said. He glanced over at Sandy, who was wringing his hands. He'd never seen Sandy flustered, and it scared him almost as much as Theresa's news had.

"Ryan. You're just a kid. You deserve to have a good life. I know you love Theresa, but she's got her own life to deal with. This baby might not even be yours. Don't throw away everything you've worked so hard for just because you feel like you owe her."

"I don't owe *her,* I owe the baby."

Sandy looked surprised. "What do you mean?"

"I never really had a father growing up," Ryan said. "My own father left us when I was a kid. Every day of my life I wondered if he left because of me, and I wished more than anything that I could see

188

him, let him get to know me, so maybe he'd realize I wasn't such a bad kid after all. I can't let that happen to this baby. Whether he's my kid or not, he deserves to have a father."

Sandy squeezed Ryan's shoulder. "Hey, kiddo, you've got a father," he said. "Me."

Ryan crumpled. Sandy's kindness was the final straw — the one that sent him over the edge. "I know," he sobbed. "It's because I've known you, and known what having a father means, that I have to do this."

Sandy had no answer for that. He just hugged Ryan and shut his eyes, hoping for the best.

Ryan and Theresa spent the next few days talking, and at breakfast on Monday morning, he made an announcement.

"Theresa's moving back to Chino. She's decided to have the baby."

The Cohens all looked at one another, waiting for the other shoe to drop.

"And —" Ryan took a deep breath — "I'm going with her." As hard as it was to say that — god, just the thought of leaving the Cohens', where he'd felt truly loved for the first time in his life, made him feel sick and dizzy. But he could see a life for this baby in Chino that would be exactly like his own childhood, and there wasn't a chance in hell he would let that happen. Not to this baby, whether it was his or not. "We're leaving right after Julie and Caleb's wedding."

"What? You can't!" Seth exclaimed angrily. He

jumped up from the table, glaring at Ryan. Then ran out of the room.

Kirsten got up to go after him. As she passed Ryan, she paused, hugging him around the neck. "You've always got a home here," she said, her eyes welling up with tears.

Ryan looked at Sandy, who shook his head. "If you need anything at all —" he started, and Ryan nodded.

"Thanks," he said.

Marissa didn't cry when Ryan told her the news. She just sat on the edge of a folding chair, surrounded by the bustling happiness of her mother's wedding, staring down at her pale hands. Ryan had wanted to tell her before the wedding that he was leaving, but the time never seemed right. He and Marissa never managed to get a second alone together, and Marissa was already so miserable about her family that Ryan didn't know how to land this final blow. Julie and Caleb had promised to help Jimmy get back on his feet financially if Marissa agreed to come live with them, and as much as Marissa hated the thought of living with her mom again, she'd do anything in the world to help her dad out. He really needed that money, and if the only way for her to get it was to sacrifice her own happiness, then that's what she'd do.

Not like she had any chance at being happy now anyway. Ryan and Theresa . . . having a baby together. Unbelievable. And even though telling her at Julie's wedding was the worst possible timing — at least he'd had the sense to wait until after the formal pictures were taken, thank god, so she wouldn't have to work even harder to manufacture a smile — in a way, it was also the best time. Now at least she had an excuse for looking so sullen on what should be a joyful occasion.

Ryan tried to think of something to say that would make her feel better, but really, there was nothing to say. Theresa was back at the Cohens', loading the last of their things in the car, and he needed to get back there so they could reach Chino before it got too late. He'd only come to the wedding to support Marissa, and he wasn't doing too good a job of that. So he didn't stay long, and when he was leaving he hugged her, but Marissa just stood limp in his arms, not hugging him back, as he murmured a final good-bye and turned and walked out of her life.

Marissa didn't even wait until he was gone before she headed to the bar. She began downing drinks, one after another. There wasn't enough alcohol in the world to numb her pain. But she was sure going to try.

When Ryan got back to the house, Theresa had her car all packed up. He changed his clothes, back into blue jeans and his leather jacket, almost exactly what he'd been wearing when he first arrived at the Cohens' door.

He went inside to say good-bye to Sandy and

Kirsten. Kirsten hugged him for five full minutes, urging him to come visit as soon as he could. And Sandy slipped him some cash and squeezed his shoulder so hard Ryan was sure he would have a bruise.

Ryan walked to the door and looked back at where they stood, Kirsten leaning on Sandy for support.

"Thank you," he said, his voice breaking. "Good-bye."

"See you soon," Sandy said, trying to make his voice jovial, and Kirsten gave a little wave.

Then Ryan headed upstairs to say good-bye to Seth. Seth was lying on his bed staring at the wall. He wouldn't even look at Ryan or at the present Ryan handed him — the map of Tahiti that he'd given Ryan when he first arrived. Finally, Ryan shouldered his bag and headed back downstairs.

Seth almost hadn't made it to the wedding. He didn't care about any of those people. Didn't care about anyone in Newport, actually, now that Ryan was going. Everything good that had happened to him over the last year, being accepted at school, the friends he'd made, Summer, all that was because of Ryan. Ryan was so cool that he made Seth seem cool simply by proximity. And he was also such a wild card that bullies were afraid to mess with Seth when they knew Ryan had his back. But who had his back now? No one.

Ryan was gone. Luke was gone — god, who

would ever have thought that there would be a world where he would actually miss Luke? He was never really friends with Marissa. And Summer . . . well, how long did he really think Summer would stay around once she realized that he'd gone back to being the geeky, unpopular weirdo he was before Ryan arrived?

No, Seth wasn't going to fool himself — there was nothing left for him in Newport now. He thought back to what he used to do before he had Ryan to hang out with, and the only thing he could remember getting any pleasure from was his schooner. He had always wanted to sail to Tahiti to escape the brutal social landscape of the O.C. Maybe he should go there now.

He looked at the map Ryan had given him, and, the more he thought about it, the more the idea appealed to him. He threw some clothes in a duffel bag, packed up a cooler in the kitchen, scribbled a quick note to his parents telling them not to worry, and a longer one to Summer, saying all the things he'd never be able to say face-to-face. Then he headed down to the marina. Maybe he wouldn't make it to Tahiti, but he could get in his boat and see where the currents took him. Anywhere would be better than here.

Theresa was waiting in the car. He got into the passenger side and stared out the window.

"Are you ready to go home?" Theresa asked him, reaching over to take his hand.

Ryan smiled at her, squeezing her hand back, but she had it wrong.

He wasn't going home, he was leaving it.

As Theresa's car pulled out, a black limo pulled into Caleb and Julie's driveway. Marissa stepped out of it. She locked eyes with Ryan, gazing at him until Theresa's car turned a corner and vanished from sight.

No, he definitely wasn't going home.

Everything's changing in the O.C.

The Newport summer scene has arrived, with days at the beach and nights spent partying. It's the same always, but it isn't. Ryan's back in Chino, Seth's sailed away to places unknown, Marissa's losing herself in alcohol, and Summer's finding a new love. Everything's changed. Nothing is the same. Can it ever be?

THE WAY BACK

Coming in December 2004

If you missed any of the action,
now you can catch up:

THE OUTSIDER

It's not who you are, it's who
they think you are.

It's the story behind the story.
There's so much more than
you're allowed to see on TV!

It's nothing like where you live.
And nothing like what you imagine.

Watch Season 2
of the O.C.
on Fox